I0607715

THE END

The Amulet Saga
Volume Seven

by

Avily Jerome

THE END
Published by Dragontail Press
PO Box 54550
Phoenix, AZ, 85078

ISBN 978-1-7321879-8-6
Copyright © 2019 by Avily Jerome
Cover art concept by Sarah Collotta
Cover design by Kirk DouPonce, Dog Eared Design

Available in print from your local bookstore, online, or from the author at:
www.avilyjerome.com

For more information on this book and the author visit: www.avilyjerome.com

All rights reserved. Non-commercial interests may reproduce portions of this book without the express written permission of the author, provided the text does not exceed 500 words. When reproducing text from this book, include the following credit line: *"The Amulet Saga, Volume Six: The Beginning* **by Avily Jerome, published by Dragontail Press. For more information visit www.avilyjerome.com. Used by permission."**

Commercial interests: No part of this publication may be reproduced in any form, stored in a retrieval system, or transmitted in any form by any means—electronic, photocopy, recording, or otherwise—without prior written permission of the author, except as provided by the United States of America copyright law.

This is a work of fiction. Names, characters, and incidents are all products of the author's imagination or are used for fictional purposes. Any mentioned brand names, places, and trademarks remain the property of their respective owners, bear no association with the author or the publisher, and are used for fictional purposes only.

Brought to you by Avily Jerome
And by Dragontail Press, www.avilyjerome.com

Library of Congress Cataloging-in-Publication Data
Jerome, Avily
The End/Avily Jerome 1st ed.

Printed in the United States of America.

Acknowledgments

Special thanks to my husband, who supports me and encourages me to pursue my passion.

Thanks also to my dad, whose continual support for my writing and my books blesses me beyond words.

Thanks to my mom, who taught me to read and instilled in me an endless love of the written word.

Thanks to my Wonder Women, who help me up when I'm down and encourage me in every step of my writing. I couldn't do this without you three.

Thank you to my readers, the ones who are still interested in what's going on in Legerdemain.

Table of Contents

The Prince 10
The Queen 14
The Sorceress 18
The Meeting 22
The Council 26
The Tunnel 32
The Spell 36
The Monster 40
The Quest 46
The Darkness 50
The Journey 56
The Cellar 62
The Tapestries 66
The Regent 72
The Canyon 78
The Seeing 82
The World 86
The Ultimatum 90
The Freed 94
The Cairn 100
The Dungeons 106
The Portal 110
The Dragons 116
The Cuff 120
The Confrontation 126
The War – Part One 130
The War – Part Two 136
The Final Battle 140
The End 146

The daughter of the dragon
Who oversees the land
Will live until the day
The dragons come again

Love she'll never know
A child she'll never have
The kings and queens of fate
Her legacy will show

From the path fate strays
The Lover and the Traitor
When the Solstice Moon shines brightly
And at the Dragon, the Dancer waves

Across the ocean wide
The darkness rises swiftly
Untold power unleashed
Building until that day

The reign of power shifts
Fate in the balance
The weight of choices made
Brings life or the end of all

The child lost arises
To take the power back
A child of the enemy
Begotten then to conquer

When the dragons rise again
When the mountains open wide
When the stones of heaven fall
The world is remade.

When the darkness reigns
Then the hate shall bind
The hearts of one and all
Until the light is found

Those who triumph fall
Those who seek shall find
Those who rule shall serve
The servant, ruler of all

The begotten of the dragons
Beloved of the Creator
Who bears the Dragon Stone
The Deliverer of the World

THE
END

The Amulet Saga
Volume Seven

The Prince

"Like this," Troy's mother said. She held the glowing ball of light aloft, making it flicker and flame, back and forth, over and over.

Troy sucked in a deep breath and closed his eyes. Everyone said this should be easy. His mother, Queen Rina, was a powerful sorceress. She'd defeated an evil king and a whole army of sorcerers in order to take back her kingdom. She'd slain magical beasts and made magical rain pour from the sky, all while pregnant with him. She was honored not only throughout Legerdemain, but in the neighboring countries, as well.

She was revered not only for her magical skill, but also her leadership.

How could any son of hers be so daft when it came to magic use? Though they never said it to his face, Troy had heard the whispers, caught the confused and even sometimes disdainful glances of those who thought he should have inherited more magical ability than he had.

He pulled the light into himself, the way his mother had explained a thousand times or more. Felt it pulsing through is veins. Let it warm him from the inside out. He pushed that feeling through his arm, to his hand, to his fingertips, and out.

A tiny flame sputtered to life and then immediately went out.

Why couldn't he do it? Everyone said magical ability was inherited, and he came from a long line of powerful magic users. So why was he so useless, no matter how many times he tried?

He huffed out a deep breath and tried again. Again, the magic sputtered and died as soon as it left his body.

His mother raised up on her toes and kissed his forehead. "That's enough for today. Have you done your other lessons?"

Troy wiped the kiss with his sleeve. At nearly sixteen years old, he was taller than she, but he would never, apparently, be old enough to avoid his mother kissing him. "I completed my history and government lessons with Sir Menden this morning. I'm going to go practice fencing with Sir Kire."

He trotted down outside to the courtyard by the stables. Sir Kire was already waiting for him. He smiled and handed Troy a long, thin sword. This style of fighting was new. The battles that had been fought in his mother's time and before were heavy, two-handed weapons. There was a legend of the first king of Legerdemain who had lost an arm in a battle against magical beasts, much like the creatures that still haunted the forest. That king was so strong, it was said he could wield a battle sword with one arm. It was said he'd killed gods with his mighty strength.

Troy didn't really believe that, though. He'd lifted those old battle swords, and they were much too heavy to use one-handed, especially against a god. Troy much preferred fighting with these new swords, where speed and agility and strategy were more effective than sheer strength.

Troy pulled a helmet over his shaggy brown hair. It was hot inside the heavy metal canister, but given the number of times Sir Kire struck him, he accepted the necessary protective gear.

Sir Kire lunged into his defensive stance, his feet wide enough to give him balance, his body angled to minimize the expanse of his body that Troy could strike.

Troy mirrored his stance and lifted his sword.

"Up a little higher. Watch where you're aiming," Sir Kire said. "Aim for my face."

Troy lifted his sword and touched it to Sir Kire's. He put just a little pressure against Sir Kire's sword so he could feel when and what direction Sir Kire moved.

So quickly Troy didn't have time to react, Sir Kire pushed Troy's sword out of the way with his own, then repositioned and thrust the blunted tip into the thickly padded tunic Troy wore, right where his heart was.

That was a kill.

"What's the first rule?" Sir Kire asked.

Troy sighed. "Don't die."

"Exactly. Again."

Again, Troy mirrored Sir Kire's stance and put pressure on his blade.

This time, when Sir Kire moved, Troy stepped back, two quick shuffles, so he was out of reach of Sir Kire's blade.

"Good!" Sir Kire said. He closed the gap between them, positioning his sword against Troy's again.

He lunged, and Troy stepped back, but Sir Kire kept attacking, prodding, until Troy pressed up against the stable wall.

Sir Kire placed the sword against Troy's throat. "Where was your mistake?"

"I—I don't know."

"You let me keep coming. You didn't fight back. You let yourself be pushed into a place where there was nowhere left to move. You must train your mind to be aware of more than one thing at a time. Be aware of my blade. Be aware of your surroundings. And start thinking ahead, plan your moves. Don't just react. Don't just defend. Learn to attack. Find a weakness and exploit it."

He stepped back to the center of the courtyard. "Again."

Troy sucked in a deep breath and faced his teacher, readying his sword.

Behind him, the castle door clanged open.

Troy turned at the sound.

"Your highness, get inside, immediately!" a page shouted, panting.

Troy looked back to Sir Kire.

"Go," he said.

Troy sprinted toward the castle. A guard barred the door as soon as he was inside.

"What's going on?" Troy asked.

"Don't know," the guard said. "Just have my orders to defend the door at all costs."

Troy bolted to the throne room, where he knew his mother would be.

He was right. She stood by the window, looking south. By her side was an old woman, the oldest woman Troy knew. His mother's advisor, Ada.

12

He hurried to join them. "What's going on?" he demanded.

His mother and Ada both turned to look at him.

"You're safe. Good," Ada said.

"Of course I'm safe. What's happening?" He was taller than both of them, and he peered over them to look outside, but saw nothing. In the distance, wisps of smoke rose from the chimneys of the houses and taverns in the South Village, and beyond that, almost imperceptible from here, the dark green line of the forest circled the kingdom.

Other than that… nothing. Nothing out of the ordinary. Nothing to make his mother or Ada stare nervously and worry for his safety. The farms and orchards that sprawled across the country looked the same as ever.

"Mother. Will you tell me what is going on?"

"We are being invaded," his mother said at last.

"By whom?"

"We don't know yet," Ada said. "But I felt it. A magic darker than any I have ever encountered is on its way here."

A cloud passed over the sun, casting a shadow over the land, as if echoing Ada's words.

The words of a prophecy ran through Troy's mind. A prophecy that had been drilled into him from the moment he was born.

When the darkness reigns
Then the hate shall bind
The hearts of one and all
Until the light is found

The Queen

Rina looked out the window, her vision enhanced by magic. Ada had Seen them coming, but not until they were within Legerdemainian borders.

It was a small entourage—smaller than Rina would have expected based on the level of threat Ada felt.

The amulet around Rina's neck seemed to burn with energy. Magic pulsed around her, filling her with the power of the threat that loomed just beyond the South Village.

"I don't see anything," Troy said, coming from behind to stand beside her.

She took his hand. He was too old for that, but she needed the comfort of feeling his warmth and the throb of his pulse beneath his skin. To know he was healthy and unharmed.

He let her maintain her grip. He would usually pull away, but he must sense her anxiety.

"They're out of sight yet, but they are coming."

"How do you know?" Troy asked.

"I can feel them," Ada said from Rina's other side. "I could not See them before. I felt the threat weeks ago, but could not tell where it was coming from or what it meant. But now... I fear the end is near."

Rina's heart clenched.

Sixteen years she'd reigned in relative peace. Sixteen years of health and prosperity for her people, rebuilding the kingdom her uncle had nearly destroyed. Wielding magic as it was meant to be used, in harmony with nature, symbiotically helping both to grow.

She had hoped to pass on a legacy to her son, but now… She didn't need Ada's warnings to tell her how bad things could get. The magic pulsing through her carried with it a darkness that told her all she needed to know.

Lighting flashed out from the now-dark sky. Not magical in origin—at least, not wielded by a person. But something felt strange about it. Something wasn't right about any of it.

"The South Village is being evacuated?" Rina asked.

"Yes," Ada said. "The other villages, too. People are being told to bring food and supplies and come within the city walls."

"Good. Send soldiers to harvest everything they can. We need to be prepared for a siege. Whoever is coming… they are more powerful than I am."

"Mother…" Troy's voice sounded choked. He lifted his chin in false bravado. "I know I disappoint you with my ability to wield magic, but I can use a sword, and I will defend this kingdom with my life."

Rina squeezed his hand. "You have never disappointed me. Do not fear. We will come through this."

She hoped her words sounded more assured than she felt. In truth, she had no idea what would happen. When she'd defeated her uncle, she didn't have a plan. She took each step as it came. She had an idea and she jumped on it, not caring about the consequences. And her lack of planning, lack of caring for what happened to anyone else had gotten Troy's father killed.

He'd tried to save her, to keep her from putting herself in harm's way, and he'd been killed in the process.

By Ada.

Rina's gaze darted to the old woman. She'd long since forgiven her advisor for her husband's death. The older Troy, for whom her son was named, had stolen the amulet Rina now wore. Ada was trying to stop a prophecy from being fulfilled. She was doing her duty to the kingdom. Rina still felt a pang whenever she thought about it, however. The first Troy had been a loyal and loving man.

She glanced at her son. Also loyal and loving, strong and steady… but she saw none of the first Troy in him.

15

She would not acknowledge, even to herself, who she did see.

"Send an emissary," she said to Ada. "See if we can gather any information about who is coming and what they want."

Ada nodded and left the room.

"We need to make a plan to keep you safe. If we are besieged, I want you far away."

"Where?"

"I don't know. Cadalania, maybe. But you'll have to go around the long way. I'll prepare a retinue for you. You will leave as soon as we find out what the danger is."

"I'm not leaving."

"I will not argue with you about this, Troy. I will defend the kingdom, but I need to know that you will be safe to rule it if something should happen to me."

"I'm not leaving," he said again.

Rina inhaled. Sweet, stubborn boy. She would put a sleeping spell on him if she had to. But she would get him out of the country. She couldn't focus on defeating her enemy if she was worried about his safety.

"We'll discuss it later. I must call the Council. We need to be prepared for anything."

Ada returned a few moments later and the three of them made their way to the Council chamber.

Servants had been sent to gather the Council members, and Rina swept down the hallway to the small, enclosed room where Council was held.

Some of them had gathered already. Sir Kire, Lady Brandys, and Lady Altya all sat at the table.

They weren't nobility in the sense that other countries defined nobility as having noble blood. No one in the history of Legerdemain had ever had truly royal blood. Even the first king was a warrior. The royal line, as it was, had been passed down through the oldest child because of the first king's vow to protect the country, not because there was anything special about his lineage.

Before Rina was born, her uncle William had slaughtered everyone of noble heritage in the kingdom, including Rina's father, the rightful heir, in an attempt to seize the throne for himself. Ada had smuggled Rina out of the castle through a servant, Margaret. Margaret had raised Rina as her own until William's men killed her.

16

When Rina defeated William and retook the throne, she had named some of her trusted followers as nobility and elevated them to the Council.

Sir Menden hurried into the room. "I'm sorry for my tardiness, Majesty," he said.

"No need to apologize," Rina smiled. "Please, be seated. We must begin as soon as possible."

"Why are we here?" Lady Brandys asked. "What has happened?"

Rina looked to Ada for explanation.

"Someone has crossed our borders," Ada said. "Someone who I believe means to do us harm. They wield powerful magic, so powerful that I could not See them beyond a vague sense of danger."

"What do they want?" Sir Kire asked.

"We do not yet know. But I fear dire times are ahead. The purpose of this Council is to determine the best course of action, both for meeting with our visitors and for keeping the prince safe."

Troy's head snapped up.

Rina's heart clenched. He looked so surprised. Could he really believe that she would let anything happen to him? Did he not know that her first priority, even above her country, would be him?

"In addition to the immediate threat," Ada went on, "I fear there are worse portents. The final prophecies are coming into play."

Rina stared at her. She had not mentioned that.

The final prophecies?

She'd studied the prophecies since becoming queen. Ada had taught her the history of Legerdemain, the kings and queens who had come before her, and how she thought each of them fulfilled a small piece of the larger prophecy spoken by the first king. The last bit, the most troubling, was yet to come.

And now Ada thought the time was at hand.

The Sorceress

Ada pored over the prophecy, the original written on parchment. How many times had she read it over her long, long life?

She'd been there when the prophecy was first spoken. She'd heard the words from the first king's mouth. He himself did not know what he'd said, but Ada had felt the weight of them from the first moment.

She'd watched over nearly a thousand years as kings had come and gone, as pieces had been fulfilled. Queen Rina had fulfilled a part—the line that stated, "A child lost arises to take the power back" was almost certainly Rina. But prophecies were funny things. That one line was nestled in with the next, which Ada was almost certain pointed to Troy, not Rina.

Like Seeing, prophecies could often only be interpreted after their fulfillment. But the prophecy spoke of a time of darkness and despair, when all hope would be lost. She couldn't say how she knew, but deep in her soul lay the assurance that this was that time.

The Age was ending, and there was nothing she could do to stop it. It would get worse before it got better, that she knew. The end of the prophecy spoke of the world being remade. Of dragons rising again. But the destruction that would come with that change…

She could only hope to save as many as she could through that ordeal.

"My lady?" Sir Kire poked his head into the Council room, where she'd lingered, hours after everyone else had gone.

She looked up.

"They are at the gates. Setting up camp. It does not yet appear to be a siege, but her Majesty would like you on hand for the negotiations."

Ada nodded and tucked the scroll into an alcove behind one of the tapestries. She followed Sir Kire down the hall and out the front door, where a horse awaited her. Queen Rina and Prince Troy were already mounted. They rode, along with a contingent of guards and soldiers, toward the wall that surrounded the city.

The streets teemed with people—refugees from the South Village, most likely—who peered out of the doorways of tents and other hastily constructed shelters as they passed.

Ada's heart constricted. Many of these people would die, and there was nothing they could do to stop it.

Leaving the horses at the gate, Ada and the queen and prince ascended the narrow stairs up to the flat rim of the wall.

Queen Rina stepped forward and looked down upon the camp that had been erected outside the walls. The amulet around her neck glowed with a faint purple light as a magical barrier grew up around her.

Ada pulled magic into herself, as well, filling herself with it and readying it for whatever purpose it might be needed. She nodded to Prince Troy, indicating that he should stay behind her, out of sight. He needed to be involved in the proceedings, to learn the art of negotiation, so he would be a competent king one day, but there was no need to put him in needless danger.

"Welcome." Queen Rina's voice rang out over the camp, enhanced by magic, but cool and calm. "What brings you to our kingdom?"

A woman stepped out from the center tent. She was tall, elegant, with deep olive skin and dark, tilted eyes. Her features seemed ageless somehow. Her eyes held the depths of age, of having seen untold ages, but her skin was smooth, her hair dark and glistening, but with a streak of silver at each temple.

She smiled at Rina. "I am looking for the sorceress called Ada."

Ada stepped forward, her eyes narrowed. How did this woman know her? She was certain she'd never seen her before. "I am Ada," she said.

The woman's smile stretched further, though her eyes were cold. "So it's true. You're still alive."

"Do I know you?" Ada asked.

19

The woman shook her head. "We've never met. But I know you. And I think you'll find you've heard of me. But even if not, I still wish to talk to you and learn from you. You have discovered the secret of everlasting life."

"You must be confused. I am not immortal."

"And yet you have lived longer than any human."

"What makes you think that?" It was true, of course. But then, Ada was not fully human. The human lifespan didn't apply to her. The magic that bound her to the land as its protector also played a part. But these were not things she could share, secrets she could impart for anyone to use. Besides, she didn't know what this woman wanted or was prepared to do to accomplish her goals.

The woman looked at her as though looking through her, reading her thoughts. "I knew someone, a long time ago, who told me about you. You were ancient two hundred years ago, and yet you still live."

Ada's heart clenched. A suspicion began to form in her mind, but she couldn't draw together all the pieces to make it fit. Two hundred years. So much had happened since then. What happened two hundred years ago that was significant? And how did it connect her to this woman? "You knew someone two hundred years ago? Then why do you need my secrets to defy age?"

"I would really prefer to discuss this over tea or wine, rather than shouting up to the top of a battlement. Will you join me in my tent?"

Queen Rina grabbed her hand. "Don't do it," she whispered. "I don't trust her."

"Neither do I. But I don't know that I have a choice. We don't know what she wants or what she's capable of. We must learn what she wants, and if we can resolve this peacefully, then we must do so."

"I'm not sure that will be possible," Queen Rina said. "I have a bad feeling about this."

"As do I. The omens all point to this being the beginning of a dark time. But I will protect you with my life, as I always have."

Ada turned to face the woman on the ground. "I will join you in your tent."

The woman nodded. "Thank you. I will have refreshments prepared."

Ada bowed. "Very well."

She stepped away from the edge and turned toward the stairs.

The woman on the ground gasped so loudly it almost sounded like a scream. Ada jerked around to see what had caused the reaction.

The woman on the ground stared up at Prince Troy, her eyes wide and filled with horror. Her mouth worked soundlessly for several moments before she choked out a single word. "Jarok?"

The Meeting

Ada waited until the queen and prince had time to reach the castle before nodding to the guards to open the gates and let her out. She pulled the amulet over her head and tucked the gem beneath her dress.

"Protect my son." The queen's words rang in her ears.

She would if she could.

But the darkness that pressed all around her sapped her of any optimism. Still, she could not let this sorceress see her despair.

She calmed her features, putting on a stoic mask, and strode purposefully a—at least as much so as her tired old bones would allow—out toward the tent where the sorceress still stood.

The sorceress smiled. "Thank you for coming. Won't you come in?"

Ada gave a slight bow and followed the woman into the tent.

"Have a seat."

Ada sat on one of the cushions that had been placed on either side of a small table. How had the sorceress gotten all this here so quickly?

Of course, the answer was in the question. She was a sorceress. All this was a display of her power. A show of superiority and strength.

The woman sat across from Ada, poured them each a cup of tea, and smiled.

And for the first time in nearly a thousand years, Ada was overwhelmed with sheer terror.

"Who are you?" she asked, pleased to find that her voice remained steady and clear. "How do you know me?"

"My name is Lysli. I am the High Consul of Oajure. I once knew one of your subjects."

Oajure.

That explained much.

Too much.

"Reith," Ada said.

Lysli smiled. "You do remember him."

"Of course. It was I who sent his betrothed to rescue him."

"And a lot of trouble that caused me," Lysli said, a laugh that sounded amused at a distant memory coloring her voice. "When he left, he took with him my greatest leverage. The wife of my worst enemy and greatest rival, and her unborn son. It took me years to undo that mess and regain control. But we're not here to talk about that.

Ada held her tea but did not drink. "What are we here to talk about?"

"You."

Ada spread her hand in a gesture of openness. "Here I am. What would you like to know?"

"How old are you?"

"I lost count of the exact years a long time ago," Ada said.

"And yet you still live, and your magic is just as strong. How do you do it?"

"It is not my doing. A long time ago, I took an oath to protect this land through this Age. The magic that binds me to my vow sustains me."

"I have never heard of magic so powerful, and believe me when I say I have searched the entire earth for it."

Ada raised an eyebrow. "The entire earth?"

Lysli nodded. "By the time Oajure was safely in hand, I was getting old. I had no heir, and no one I trusted enough to share my secrets with. I considered allowing Reith to sire my heir. His magical ability was unlike any I'd ever seen. He was strong. Strong enough to break free from my control, which was no easy feat. He was of the royal family, yes? Tell me about them."

Ada weighed her response carefully. This woman knew so much already. Any information might give her the edge she needed to accomplish her goals. And yet refusing to cooperate might anger her, and Ada needed time to find out what she wanted, as well as come up with a plan to counter whatever she had in mind.

23

Besides, talking would give her as much insight as it would Lysli.

She took the tiniest sip of the tea, savoring it, trying to determine whether there were any ingredients that would impair her ability to use magic.

There was nothing she could identify, but she still wouldn't drink more than a sip.

She smiled at Lysli. "The royal line is not royal, in the strictest sense. Our first king was just a man. A refugee. He earned the respect of his people through his bravery and wisdom and self-sacrifice. He was unanimously voted to be the king. Through magic and a sacred vow, his heirs have kept the throne throughout the years."

"Interesting. And they are all gifted in magic?"

"To some extent, although of course some are more powerful than others."

Except Troy. Not that she'd let on to this sorceress that despite the untold hours she had spent in training, Troy showed almost no magical aptitude. It didn't matter—he was still the heir.

"The boy with you on the parapet," Lysli said.

Ada's heart stuttered. Had the sorceress been planning to bring him up all along, or was she somehow sensing Ada's thoughts?

"What about him?" Ada asked.

"Who is he?"

"Why does it matter?"

"He looks like someone I once knew. I realize now it cannot be the same person—the man I knew died many years ago. I know, because I killed him. But he had a son."

"The one you spoke of before. The unborn son of your rival."

Lysli nodded. "Jarok the Eleventh. He was a powerful sorcerer. His son would've been equally powerful, as would all his descendants. The boy on the parapet is the very image of him. He would be… how many generations, do you suppose, from the Jarok I knew? I'm guessing that boy is Jarok the Twenty-first or so."

"That is not his name."

"Perhaps not, but that doesn't mean that's not who he is. Who are his parents?"

"His father was one of the queen's guards."

"And his mother?"

"The queen."

"So the queen's guard could have been descended from Jarok, then."

24

Ada smiled and took another perfunctory sip of her tea. "The people of Legerdemain are made up of the descendants of people of every land. This country was started as a place of refuge for those seeking to escape the Great War. Any resemblance you see to anyone you used to know is purely happenstance."

"I see. So, that boy is not the most powerful sorcerer in the land?"

Ada smiled again, thankful for the first time that Troy's abilities were so limited. The sorceress would be able to tell if Ada were lying—she would sense the disturbance in the magical energies. But in this, she had nothing to lie about. Troy would be safe from further prying.

"He is not. He has almost no magical ability whatsoever."

Lysli's eyes bored into Ada for a long moment, and Ada knew she was trying to catch any hint of deception.

At last, Lysli leaned back and the smile overtook her features once again. "Then he is of no consequence to me. Let us discuss the real reason for my visit."

Visit. What a lovely term for invasion.

Ada smiled. "And that is?"

"I will rule this land. I have already taken control of the lands to the south and west. You are no match for my powers, even as powerful as you are. You will either surrender to me and be absorbed into my empire peacefully, or I will take this land by force."

A pulse of magic thrummed out from Lysli. Nothing that would hurt anyone—yet. Just a wave to let Ada know exactly how much magic she could wield, a warning against any attempt to fight back.

"I'll let you discuss it with your queen. I expect an answer in three days. You may go."

A cloud of dark red smoke surrounded Lysli, obscuring her, and when it dissipated, Lysli was gone and Ada was alone in the tent.

Ada stood and marched back toward the castle wall. This was not going to go well.

The Council

Troy had stared at the woman below him, his mouth dry, when she'd called him Jarok. He'd heard the name, of course. There were rumors about a man named Jarok who had worked for his mother's uncle, the previous king. Jarok was reputed to be a powerful sorcerer, the man responsible for creating the monsters that lived in the forest.

A few of the creatures were still presumed to be alive, wandering the woods. Runaway cattle and other animals were said to be victims of the beasts. But the road in and out of the kingdom had been safe since his mother began her reign.

Other rumors were whispered about Jarok, and how Queen Rina had used him then defeated him. Troy had heard things, but his mother always assured him the stories were nothing but lies.

But why would the strange sorceress think he was Jarok?

He and his mother had raced from the wall to the castle, Queen Rina almost pushing him over multiple times in her hurry to get him home.

Troy turned as he reached the gate to see his mother running behind him. "Inside. Now!"

She shoved in behind him. "Bar the door," she told the guard. "Send a servant to call the Council members.

She grabbed Troy's hand and ran toward the Council chambers.

"Mother, what's going on?" Troy asked.

"Council room. Now," Queen Rina said, breathless.

Troy followed her, his heart thumping in his chest. "What about Ada?"

"Ada will be fine," she said.

Troy glanced again at her. The amulet was missing from around her neck. She must have given it to Ada to use.

Queen Rina pushed into the Council room behind him and shoved the door closed, barring it from the inside.

"How will the Council get in if it's locked?" Troy asked.

"I'll let them in when they come," the queen said.

"Mother..." Troy paused before asking the question. He already knew the only possible answer. He knew there was only one reason. And yet he needed to hear it. Needed his mother to say it out loud. "What is going on? Why did that woman think I am Jarok?"

Queen Rina took a deep breath and looked at him, as though weighing whether or not to tell him the truth. At last, she nodded slowly. "There's a chance your father was not who I believed him to be. It's possible your father was Jarok, the sorcerer who worked for my uncle."

Troy nodded. "Why did you lie about it all these years?"

"Because I didn't want it to be true. Jarok and I had a... connection. A magical force that drew us together. And yes, I used that connection to manipulate him. It was the only way I could see to get close to the king in order to bring him down."

The thought of his mother using her feminine wiles or whatever she had done to seduce and coerce someone sent a shudder through Troy, but he pushed the feeling aside. This was not the time to worry about that. A sorceress stood at their door, and she knew the truth.

"How did she know? That woman, I mean?"

"I don't know. She said she knew someone who knew Ada two hundred years ago. She must have known Jarok at some point, too."

"How is that possible? Does she use the same kind of magic Ada uses to keep from getting old?"

"I don't know. I don't know how Ada does it, either. But I don't believe it is the same. Ada is unique, and her motives are pure. This woman... I could feel the evil rolling off her. However she does it, it's not like Ada."

"Then we need to figure out how she's doing it and stop her."

"We will do no such thing. You will stay inside, protected by guards and sorcerers at all times, and not give that woman a chance to do anything to harm you."

"Mother, you can't protect me forever. This is my kingdom, too. It's time I started acting like a protector of this land rather than a baby of it."

His mother opened her mouth to respond, but before she had a chance to speak, someone banged on the door. "Your Majesty, it is Sir Kire and Lady Altya. Please let us in."

"Step back," the queen said.

Troy obeyed, standing to the side so his mother could ease the door open and check to make sure it really was Sir Kire and Lady Altya.

She stepped aside to allow them entry, then quickly closed and barred the door again.

"Your Majesty, what is happening?" Lady Altya asked.

Troy couldn't help but notice the way Lady Altya's flush made her look radiant. He shoved the thought aside and focused on his mother's words.

"There is an army outside the walls, led by a sorceress more powerful than any I have ever seen. Possibly even more powerful than Ada."

Lady Altya gasped. "How... how is that possible? Ada is..."

"I know," Queen Rina said. "I'm more afraid because of Ada's reaction than anything. I've never seen her afraid, but today..."

She shook her head and looked at her Council members. "We must come up with a plan of action. I do not trust this sorceress. I fear for our country. And she is already within our borders with her army. We cannot use the tactics our ancestors did to keep invaders out."

Sir Kire took his seat at the table and motioned for the others to do so, as well.

Troy was the first to sit, then Lady Altya. Troy jerked his gaze away before Lady Altya could see him staring.

A knock sounded at the door, and Queen Rina let Lady Brandys and Sir Menden inside. She sat at her place at the head of the table, regal and controlled, though Troy could see her hands quivering as she clutched her skirt.

"We are here to discuss a plan of action. Our city is besieged—or it will be soon—by foreign invaders led by a powerful sorceress."

"What do they want?" Sir Menden asked.

28

"I don't know yet. Ada is talking to the sorceress now. But I fear the worst."

"So the first plan of action must be to get them out of our country," Sir Menden said. "Either by defeating them in battle or negotiating a treaty."

"We must prepare for battle," Queen Rina said. "Of course, we will attempt to negotiate first, but the sorcerers and soldiers must be ready if negotiations fail."

"Very good," Sir Menden said, scratching his notes on a piece of parchment. "And what are we prepared to give up, in terms of negotiation, for peace?"

"Gems—as many as we can, although the mines have been nearly dry for a generation or more. Crops. We don't have much else to offer. But we must see what they want. And above all, we must protect the prince."

All eyes turned to look at Troy.

"I don't need to be protected, Mother. Let me fight, just as everyone else will do, including you."

"Troy, you are the last hope for this kingdom. You…"

Troy held up his hand to silence her. "I can't even use magic. If the kingdom is going to end, then protecting me won't matter, and if it going to be saved, then all of us must do…" he paused, his head growing dizzy.

"All of us must do our…"

Darkness clouded his vision, and his breath felt tight in his chest.

"Must do our part," he wheezed before toppling to the floor.

He knew he was still in the Council room. Was vaguely aware that his mother was kneeling over him, shouting his name, and that the others had begun to crowd around him. But he was somewhere else.

A mountain.

Birds and animals chittered around him, as though not seeing him. Some invisible force pulled at him and he took a step. Walking slowly, he pushed through the trees until he came to a clearing. Monumental stone pillars marked the borders of the clearing, and in the center stood a huge stone slab.

He stepped into the clearing and toward the stone slab. As he arrived, the earth shook, and the stone wavered.

The stone moved, like the lid of a basin being slid away, revealing a gap that led into a dark tunnel.

29

Troy gasped and sat up, the dark tunnel disappearing and the Council room coming into focus.

"Troy!" his mother said, tears streaming down her face. "What happened? Are you all right?"

He looked at her. "I know what I must do."

The Tunnel

The sorceress didn't wait.

Ada felt the magic building before she even returned to the gate.

Lysli struck her from behind, a spell Ada didn't recognize, the magic powered by a language she hadn't heard for an Age.

She erected a barrier just as the spell struck, a protective shield that kept the spell from penetrating. Turning, she channeled her protection spell through the amulet around her neck to strengthen it, but even still, Lysli's spell bore down on her.

Lysli walked slowly toward her, a smile that seemed to be a strange mix of bemusement and frustration playing across her painted lips, her already angled eyes narrowing further.

"Interesting," she said, though her voice sounded strained.

Ada pulled more magic into herself, through the amulet, and wove a thread of it in a counterspell.

The spell was weak—just a sliver of lightning. It easily would've killed someone, and possibly anyone standing near, if it had been at full strength, but Ada could only spare a trickle of magic. Still, it was enough to jolt Lysli and make her lose her concentration. Lines formed around her eyes, almost looking like age lines rather than lines of concentration.

"How are you doing that?" Lysli asked, taking a step forward. "I have never met anyone who could withstand this spell. The most powerful sorcerers in the world succumbed after a few moments."

Ada didn't bother to answer. She pushed as much magic as she could into her protection spell and ran toward the gate.

The gate swung open for her.

Lysli bellowed in rage, and the magic built again, but this time it was not directed at Ada.

One of the guards stationed at the top of the wall groaned, clutched his heart, and toppled off the side.

Ada dashed the last few steps into the city within the wall and slammed the door shut. She redirected her spell so instead of just covering her, it covered the entirety of the wall. It was weaker now, but it offered some protection, at least.

She set the spell to remain even without her actively maintaining it. That made it weaker still—it would only be a matter of time until Lysli was able to break through—but hopefully it would be enough for her to warn the queen.

"Horse," she gasped.

One of the guards handed her the reins to his horse and helped her up.

She looked down at him. "Stay out of sight if at all possible. Get the archers to the wall and kill anyone who comes into view. They will slaughter us all if they can. Take out as many as you can before they do."

The guard nodded and ran to the guard house at the base of the wall. Ada turned and galloped toward the castle.

The door to the castle was locked and barred. Good. That meant Queen Rina was taking the threat seriously. She pounded until the guard at the door recognized her and let her in.

Once inside, the servants helped her to make her way to the Council room. She pounded on the door.

Her knock was echoed by a rumbling that shook the whole castle.

So soon.

She thought she'd have a little more time.

The door swung open, and Queen Rina stared from her place at the head of the table, her eyes wide with fear.

"Gather the army and all the sorcerers," Ada panted. "We're being attacked."

"Troy, stay here and don't move," Queen Rina said. "Bar the door. I'll post guards and a sorcerer, but whatever happens, do not come out."

"Mother, I have to," Troy said. "I have to go to the mountains."

"No! You have to stay safe!"

Ada looked from one to the other. What had happened while she was talking to the sorceress? What did Troy hope to find in the mountains?

"Ada, reason with her," Troy said. "I'll be safer outside the city anyway, and I have a mission. I saw it in a vision."

Ada snapped her attention to him. He had Seen? Without using a spell? Times truly were changing. "What did you See?"

"Myself, walking to the top of a mountain, far to the north. There was a clearing, surrounded by large stone pillars, with a monument in the center. I walked up to the monument, and it opened. I was supposed to go inside."

Ada's chest tightened.

She was right, then. This was the end. And Troy had a vital role to play. But Rina would not see it, and they didn't have time to argue.

Ada turned to the queen. "Let me have a moment with the boy."

Queen Rina nodded, but her eyes remained wary.

Ada removed the amulet from her neck and handed it to the queen. "You will need this. If you can link your magic with the others, you might stand a chance of weakening her, but be wary. She gains more power every time she kills."

Queen Rina and the others left the room and Ada closed the door.

"Ada, please—" Troy began.

Ada held up a hand to silence him. "I know. You're going. You'll find a way out one way or the other and your mother can't stop you."

He heaved a sigh. "Yes. So you'll help me?"

Ada nodded.

"I will send servants to bring you food. Bread and dried meat and fruit, enough to last you several days, and some extra clothes and supplies. I will tell them it is in case you must stay hidden until the end of the siege."

Troy looked at her, waiting for her next instruction.

Good. He was patient and wise. This would serve him well in his quest.

Ada turned to face the wall. "Have you seen these tapestries?"

"Of course. I'm in here all the time."

Ada nodded. "Yes, but have you ever really looked at them? Do you know what they are?"

"They're our history."

"Yes." She pointed to the first tapestry, the one with a host of huge, brilliantly colored winged beasts. "The dragons who helped found the country."

The next, a one-armed man with a sword and a crown. "Legerdemain's first king." A woman with golden hair and blue eyes stood next to the king. "And me."

Troy sucked in his breath. "You? I knew you were old, but... how?"

"You will find the answer to that question in the cavern at the top of the mountain."

"How will I get there if I cannot leave this room?"

Ada pulled aside the tapestry to reveal the stone wall behind it. She pulled a stone from the wall near the floor. The wall groaned and a small door swung back, revealing a staircase that disappeared into darkness far below. "I was here when this castle was built. No one knows about this tunnel except for me, not even your mother. It has never been used. It leads to a room inside the wall, along the north edge. A small door will lead you outside the castle."

Troy threw his arms around her in a tight embrace. "Thank you."

"Don't thank me yet. You may yet decide you would've been better off staying here."

Troy grinned. "At least this way I have a chance to help."

"Indeed. You may be the only one who can. Remember, wait until after I send provisions. By then it will be dark and you can sneak away unnoticed. I will do my best to buy you time until then."

Ada opened the door to the hallway. Queen Rina stood there with two guards and two sorcerers.

"The prince has agreed not to come out this door until you tell him it's safe," Ada said.

Troy nodded his agreement.

"Thank you," Queen Rina said. She looked at Troy. "Bar the door."

"I will," he said.

"I promised I would send a servant with enough food to last several days and a blanket and candles and so forth," Ada said. "Then, even if the sorceress makes it inside the castle, he will be safe."

The Spell

The barrier still held, but it was getting weaker. The sorceress seemed to tirelessly barrage it with her spells, looking for weaknesses, but ultimately chipping away at it, rocking the whole city with every burst of magic she launched at it..

Ada and the queen joined the sorcerers and soldiers who gathered atop the city wall. Some of them bolstered the protective shield, while others aimed spells at the camp below, setting tents afire and sending earthquakes to disrupt the army, but Lysli had put her own protections in place, and all their efforts accomplished little.

It was a standoff, and Lysli was stronger, even than Ada and Rina and all the queen's sorcerers combined. She would win. It was only a matter of time.

Ada just had to make sure it was enough time for the prince to get out and get to the mountains.

The sun sank in the west, and the castle wall cast its shadow over Ada and the queen.

Sir Kire stepped close to Ada, out of the queen's hearing. "I assume the prince is escaping?"

Ada looked at him, keeping her face expressionless.

"We all heard what he said about the vision he had. I know enough about magic to know that Seeing something like that is a dire omen that must be obeyed. And I know you would do anything to protect this country, and his vision is the best chance at doing that. With your permission, I would like to go with him to help and protect him."

Ada searched his face. He and Sir Menden had been the closest Prince Troy had to a father figure as he grew up. Rina was a good queen and a good mother, but right now, there was too much at stake. If Troy didn't succeed, the whole kingdom would be swept up in Lysli's grasp.

She trusted Sir Kire. What was more, Troy trusted him.

"He will be leaving by the north wall after dark. It will be many days' travel. Take supplies. And hurry. There is no telling what will happen here while you're gone."

"Thank you." With that, Sir Kire dashed away, heading back toward the castle.

Ada turned her attention to the sorcerers at the top of the wall.

"Ada," a sing-song voice wafted over the wall.

Lysli.

"Ada, where are you? We both know it's over. Come, let us negotiate the terms of your surrender."

"We won't surrender," Queen Rina growled.

They wouldn't have a choice. But Ada didn't say anything. The important thing now was to make it last as long as possible.

"Use the amulet to create a protection spell around me," Ada instructed.

Queen Rina followed Ada up the stairs and sat just out of sight to create her protection spell as Ada stepped into view.

"State your terms," Ada called down.

"I already gave you my terms," Lysli said.

"Yes, and then you betrayed them by attacking me as soon as I turned around. You gave us the option to be absorbed peacefully into your empire or be taken by force, but gave me no opportunity to relay your message to my queen. You have proven yourself to be untrustworthy, and so there will be no surrender. Nothing you do is peaceful. You will be destroyed."

"I assure you, I have no need of a peaceful surrender. Taking this land will be my pleasure."

"You have no idea what our powers are. Our strength. Ours is a magical land, and we are connected to it. You will never defeat us."

Lysli laughed.

"Your Majesty," Ada said softly.

"Yes?" Queen Rina's voice sounded strained from the effort of the spell.

"I don't know how long we can hold her off. But with the amulet, you might be able to do some damage. When I give the word, drop the protection spell and channel everything you can into destroying the sorceress."

Queen Rina nodded and took a step closer, staying out of sight, until she could peek ove the edge and see the sorceress below.

"Are you ready?" Ada asked.

"Yes," Queen Rina said.

Ada pulled magic into herself, through the handful of gemstones she kept on her person, and readied her own spell.

She launched a barrage of lightning at Lysli.

Lysli howled—rage and pain echoed across the valley. She turned the full force of her wrath at Ada.

"Now!" Ada hissed at Queen Rina.

Rina dropped the protection spell, and Lysli's spell hit Ada. Pain ripped through her, feeling as though her skin were being flayed from her bones and her blood was being boiled. And slowly, but not slowly enough, the magic flowing through her drained away... rushing straight to Lysli.

Not to attack her, but to fuel her.

Ada gritted her teeth and continued to pull the magic through her. As long as Lysli was focused on her, Queen Rina stood a chance.

The pain made Ada's knees buckle. The life force drained from her, and with every heartbeat, she could feel Lysli getting stronger. "Now!"

Queen Rina launched a wave of magic at Lysli through the amulet, a spell that should burn her to ash from the inside out.

Should.

Lysli dropped the spell she was using against Ada and turned it toward Queen Rina. She grabbed the magic that pulsed out from the queen through the amulet and absorbed it, then turned it around and fired it back at the queen.

Queen Rina gasped, not even able to scream, before her skin began to bubble and char. She slumped over on the wall, her features contorted in an expression of horror for a brief instant before she burned completely.

Within seconds, her body was nothing more than a mound of black ash, atop which sat the amethyst amulet, glinting violet with the last rays of the setting sun.

Ada snatched the amulet and stuffed it in a hidden pouch inside her dress. She would have to hide it—it must not fall into Lysli's hands. In the past, the amulet had destroyed those who tried to use it without being of the royal bloodline or having authorization from the ruling heir. But Ada had never seen anyone this powerful. She didn't know enough about the kind of magic that Lysli used to know whether it was more powerful than the magic that fueled the Legerdemainian line.

The amulet could not be risked.

Below, Lysli laughed.

Ada peered over the edge of the wall. The sorceress looked... younger. More vibrant. Her dark hair glistened in the torchlight that now illuminated her camp.

"Your queen was powerful," she said. "I had no idea what I'd be gaining." Her voice echoed across the valley. "Her power is now mine. I am the Empress, and you will all bow before me."

She swept her hand up, clearing the remnants of the barrier from around the city wall.

She thrust another spell at the gate, sending it flying inward and breaking it into shards.

With a wave of her hand, she summoned her army behind her and marched into the city.

A contingent of guards tried to stop her. With a sweep of her hand, she drained the first of them of life, consuming his energy, as she had done to Queen Rina. Then the next, and the next, until they stopped attacking.

Ada gasped as the realization hit her.

She'd heard of this spell, though she'd never seen it in person. But how? It was impossible. No one had used it in an Age. How did Lysli know what it was or how to do it?

This spell was used in the last Age by the gods, each of whom had hoped to kill all the others and rule the earth for eternity. It was supposed to have died with them.

So how did Lysli now use it?

The Monster

Troy emerged from the stone wall, a pack strapped to his back. He snuffed the candle that had guided him through the long tunnel beneath the city from the Council room to the door in the wall.

The door swung closed behind him, leaving the wall looking as it always had, no trace of the hidden passage to be seen.

He looked all around—he might need the entrance again—but he couldn't figure out how to open it from this side. On the inside, it had been a lever, but here—no hidden stones that came out, no secret levers or buttons. Perhaps it could only be opened from the inside.

Far away, on the other side of the city, the screams of battle rose up into the air.

His time was short. He had to get out of sight, to the mountains, before anyone noticed he was missing.

He took one last glance at the wall, then turned and began the hike toward the mountains. He angled right, a path that would take him around the North Village rather than through it. He couldn't afford to be seen.

"Your Highness."

He stopped, his heart thunking to his stomach.

Turning slowly, he faced Sir Kire, who sat atop a horse, his face grim.

"Sir Kire, I... You see, I..."

"You're going to the mountains. I know. But it will be faster on horseback." Sir Kire nodded his head toward a second horse that Troy hadn't seen.

"You mean..."

"I'm coming with you," Sir Kire said. "Let's go. There is no time to waste. Oh, and here. You may need this."

Sir Kire extended Troy's sword to him, hilt first.

Troy grinned. If he could've asked anyone to join him, it would've been Sir Kire. More than a mentor, more than a friend—Sir Kire was like family. There was no one he trusted more. And having company for the journey... he hadn't realized how much he would appreciate having the other man there until he appeared. He sheathed the sword and mounted his horse.

Without another word, Sir Kire led the way along the same trajectory Troy had begun, northeast, around the North Village and toward the mountains.

They didn't stop until they reached the treeline.

"Be careful," Sir Kire said. "We don't know if the rumors are true, but there may still be monsters living here. Even so, I suggest we get through the forest and into the mountains before we stop to rest."

Troy nodded, his stomach clenching at the thought.

The monsters were legendary. It had always seemed like a fun story to tell to scare his friends for a good thrill, but now that he was here, facing them himself...

"What about the horses?" he asked.

"We may yet need them," Sir Kire said. "It will be slow going through the forest, but they will be useful on the other side. Besides, they will hear and smell any danger long before we do."

Troy nodded. He took a deep breath, and nudged the horse forward, beyond the first trees.

The horse reared, whinnying and balking.

"Come on. It's not that bad," Troy said. "Just a little dark."

The horse took a tentative step forward. Sir Kire's horse followed, also seeming skittish, but a little more willing to venture in behind.

Darkness shrouded them. The faint light of the half moon did little to dispel the shadows that covered everything. Underbrush crunched beneath the horses' hooves, the only sound in the otherwise deathly still night. Not even a cricket chirped or a night bird cooed.

For several long minutes, they tramped through the dark, trees scraping them all along the way. Somewhere there were paths that the miners had used in generations past, but they had mostly overgrown once the mines dried up and mining stopped being profitable.

"How wide is the forest?" Troy asked. His whisper sounded like a harsh scraping in the night.

"Here?" Sir Kire's voice sounded low and guttural, like an animal. "I have no idea. Along the southern border, it's a few miles wide in some places. But up here, so close to the mountain, probably less. Maybe a mile, I'd guess."

One mile. That should take them, what, maybe half an hour, trudging along at this pace? How long had it been?

Not long enough.

The night closed in around them, wrapping them as though in a blanket. Or a shroud.

They rode in silence again, the only sound the crunching of hooves on dead leaves and the swishing of branches as they brushed past.

Something growled.

The horses both screamed, kicking and bucking, racing forward, away from the sound.

Troy fought to hold on as his horse dashed through the forest, zig-zagging between the trees.

He wasn't sure if Sir Kire was still behind him, and he had no idea what direction they were now traveling. For all he knew, they could be headed right back toward Legerdemain.

The thing growled again, sounding closer this time, sending the horse into a renewed frenzy.

The horse threw him, and he tumbled to the ground, rocks and twigs stabbing into him as he rolled, finally landing in a shrub of some sort.

The monster growled again, this time even closer.

A shriek rose from the horse, then cut off in a gurgle. The sounds of flesh ripping and blood splattering echoed in Troy's ears.

He held his breath, willing the thundering of his heart to slow down, to not thud so loudly in the night.

The slavering sounds of the monster devouring the horse slowed to a steady gnawing, punctuated by an occasional grunt.

If the beast was satisfied, perhaps he could escape.

If he had any idea which way to go.

He listened for any sound other than the monster enjoying its meal. The other horse, Sir Kire, an animal—anything.

But nothing besides the slobbering and chewing reached his ears.

He had to move. Had to get away while the beast was still distracted. Had to get out of the forest while he still had a chance.

Looking up, he searched the sky for any sign of the moon or stars that could guide him in the right direction, but leaves and shadows obscured any possible view.

Still, he had to move. If he stayed here, he would be found before long, either by this monster or another.

He rolled so he could get his knees under him. His limbs burned from a thousand bruises, and his skin stung from an infinite number of cuts and scratches from his fall.

All the more reason to escape, before the scent of fresh blood attracted more predators.

He pushed himself to his feet and stood still as a wave of dizziness threatened to overtake him. But he didn't have time to pause any longer. He made his best guess for the right direction, based on which way he thought they were moving when the horse threw him, and took a step, then another, disentangling himself from the undergrowth.

Too loud. His movements shook the forest, and somewhere behind him, the beast stopped chewing.

Troy stopped, holding his breath.

The chewing started again, and he took another step, careful to be as silent as possible. One cautious step at a time, he put some distance between himself and the beast.

When he could only faintly hear the thing eating, he risked moving a little faster, then faster still, though still much too slowly.

He took a step, his foot landing on a dry stick. The stick crunched, a loud crack breaking the stillness of the night.

The beast stopped eating. Its growl echoed through the forest. Then, the sound of its heavy footfalls on the dry leaves echoed through the forest.

Troy ran.

Branches slapped his face and roots and sticks threatened to trip him with every step, but still he ran.

Not fast enough.

The thing behind him gained with every step, crashing through the trees behind him.

43

Above, the faintest glimmer of light made the shadows less overpowering, and a sliver of gray moonlight filtered through the canopy.

Did that mean the trees were thinning? Could the edge of the forest be near?

He redoubled his efforts.

Still too slow.

The beast was right behind him.

It growled, its hot breath brushing the hairs on the back of his neck.

Then it pounced, heavy paws thudding in to his back, pushing him forward, onto his face.

A string of saliva dripped onto his head.

The Quest

The monster stopped. Sniffed.

Whined.

Stepped back off Troy.

Troy rolled over.

The beast stood above him, its head cocked, its mouth open in a snarl that revealed fangs as long as Troy's hand.

So why wasn't it eating him?

It looked... confused, if a ravenous beast could be said to have such emotions.

Troy edged up onto his arms and pushed with his feet, getting a little distance from the thing.

It took a step closer, and he raised an arm in front of his face. Blood dripped from a gash below his elbow.

The monster sniffed the blood, whined again, and backed away.

Troy stood and waved his bloody arm at the beast.

It growled, but stepped back.

Troy didn't stop to question why, he just took the opportunity to turn and run.

The monster followed, but didn't give chase. Troy heard its footfalls thudding behind him, close enough to keep him in sight but not attack. More like it was curious to see where he went, but afraid to get too near.

A few minutes later, the trees began to thin, and shortly after that, the ground began to rise. He pushed his aching body the final few steps out of the forest and up the slope of the mountain.

He'd made it. On the correct side, no less.

Now, he just had to find Sir Kire—if he still lived—and figure out which direction he was supposed to travel to find the cave.

Trudging a little more slowly with every step, he pushed on up the mountain, calling out for Sir Kire, listening for any sound of movement.

The sun edged over the horizon, soon bathing the mountainside in a rosy glow. The shadows of the sparse trees offered a little comfort as the day grew warmer, but the heat of the sun would soon be unbearable.

And he was tired. So tired. Every part of his body screamed at him to rest. But he couldn't find Sir Kire. Had the monster—or another one like it—gotten him? Had he gone the wrong way when they'd gotten separated? He had to keep looking.

But maybe he could just sit for a little bit first. He still had his pack, fully stocked with provisions that Ada had instructed the servants to bring him.

He pulled out the blanket and spread it under a tree, then took some dried fruit and meat and his water skin. He sat with his back to the tree, where he could look down at the forest's edge and watch for any sign that Sir Kire had made it out.

His eyes drifted closed and head lolled. He managed to jerk awake long enough to finish eating, but he couldn't stay alert any longer, and he allowed himself to rest.

It was evening when he woke. Normal sounds—birds and insects and the rustling of small game—filled the air. So different from inside the forest, where nothing except monsters seemed to live.

"Sir Kire?" he called out softly.

No answer.

If Sir Kire was alive, he would have emerged from the forest by now. He'd be pacing along the edge looking for Troy, and he surely would have seen the trail of blood and trampled foliage that Troy had left in his wake as he escaped the forest.

That meant Sir Kire was dead. Probably mauled by the monster.

A shock of loss mingled with terror shot through him. He was alone. His one friend gone. His home and his people under siege by a sorceress. No one knew where he was or that he was gone, which meant they weren't holding out hope that he'd return with help.

And he didn't even know what help he was supposed to bring. What was he supposed to do when he reached the cave? Would he have to open it, or would it open on its own?

But he was stalling. He needed to get moving.

He ate a little more of the food in his pack and stood. His body hurt more now than it had when he'd fallen asleep. Every limb felt twice its weight, and everything was stiff, sending jolts of agony through him every time he moved.

Sucking in a deep breath, he wadded up the blanket and stuffed it back in his pack, then began his hike.

The sun finished setting, leaving the mountainside dim. At least here the trees were thin enough that the light from the moon and stars gave him a little guidance.

Somewhere up ahead, he heard the sound of water. A stream?

The sound got louder the further he walked. Good. He needed to refill his waterskin and wash off the blood and grime from the forest.

It took longer to reach than he'd anticipated, and it was well into the night by the time he reached the stream. It was more than a stream, however, and rushing too fast and too deep to try crossing in the dark.

So once again, he pulled out his blanket and allowed himself a little rest.

He rose just after dawn and walked along the bank for a little while, heading upstream, but eventually decided to rest for the night. In the morning, he found a place with rocks big enough to stand on, and crossed the stream.

Looking back, he could see the valley far below. The ring of trees, the vast farmland, then city in the direct center of the country. The castle in the middle seemed to be no more than a speck, much too far to make out any details, let alone determine whether the castle was still besieged.

He paused to catch his breath, staring down at the castle.

What was he doing? Where was he going? He didn't really have a plan. All he knew from his vision was "up". High in the mountains, beyond the trees, lay the cave. But there were dozens of mountains. Which one had the cave? How many days of travel, going up one mountain and down the other side, then up the next, until he found it? Would he have to travel each mountain back and forth? What if he checked the wrong place, and the cave was a mile from where he went, and he never found it?

He was trusting instinct alone to guide him. But he'd felt nothing since the vision itself. He was wandering aimlessly, on a mission that he didn't even know for sure was necessary. Perhaps he should go home and fight like a soldier. Protect his country like the prince he was.

Glancing up, he looked for the top of the mountain. How many days would it take to reach the summit? And from there would he be able to tell the right direction?

He wished Sir Kire were there. At least he'd have someone to talk to. Someone to discuss all this with. To help him determine the right way. To keep him from going insane.

He glanced down again, back toward the castle.

Something down there glowed, a bright spot of red. Something—like a ruby or garnet—reflecting the sun, perhaps?

No, no gemstone in the world would be large enough to reflect such a bright light at this distance.

What, then?

The red glow intensified, growing brighter and brighter, until it consumed the castle.

It now looked like fire, but not like any fire he had ever seen. The fire blazed, pulsing out for a long moment, before being extinguished.

A black cloud formed over where the light had been, growing larger and larger, and expanding from the castle.

What could it be? A spell? And if so, what did it mean?

A shadow fell on him, and someone stepped in front of him, blocking his view.

The Darkness

As soon as the queen was dead, the battle had turned. If it could've ever been considered a battle.

The sorceress was inside the gates, and those who tried to stop her succumbed to her spell.

Ada ordered a surrender. With any luck, not everyone would die.

The soldiers and sorcerers retreated to the castle, but Ada stayed behind. Perhaps Lysli could be negotiated with.

Lysli and a contingent of sorcerers wearing dark red robes stalked through the now open gate.

Ada met her in the courtyard and bowed. "Welcome to your new kingdom, your Majesty."

Lysli sneered at her and raised her hand. She attempted the same spell that killed Queen Rina. The life ebbed from Ada, but the effort cost Lysli more energy than she gained from it. Her radiant skin faded and tiny wrinkles appeared around her eyes.

She stopped the spell, the sneer turning to irritation. "How are you doing that?" she asked again. She'd said the same thing before, right before she'd killed the queen. But Ada still wasn't sure what she meant.

"Doing what?" Ada asked.

"Stopping me from killing you."

Ada raised an eyebrow. "If I knew, I would hardly tell you, would I?"

Lysli snorted. "Very well. You will serve me, for as long as you live." She waved her hand at one of the soldiers, stealing his life and restoring her vigor.

"Yes, your Majesty. I serve the Kingdom of Legerdemain, no matter who is on the throne. I always have. Come, I will show you to your rooms."

Lysli eyed her a moment, as though not sure what to make of her compliance. "Very well." She nodded toward her entourage. "The cuff."

One of the men stepped forward and handed Lysli a silver cuff with gemstones inlaid in it. Lysli indicated to Ada to hold out her ankle.

Ada complied. She didn't have another choice at the moment.

Lysli fastened the cuff around her ankle. The amethyst in it sparked to life, burning brightly for a moment, before fading back to being just a stone.

"Curious," Lysli said. She turned to her guards. "Stay close to me. If anyone tries anything, kill them."

The sorcerers in their robes bowed to her and circled around, following Ada as she led the way to the castle.

Upon seeing Ada, the guards inside opened the gates.

"What... what is happening?" one of the guards asked as he let them in.

"We have surrendered. Queen Rina is dead. Empress Lysli is our new ruler."

She lifted her head and led the way to the queen's rooms.

"May I ask what you have planned?" Ada asked as they walked. "You said you are empress of the world. Legerdemain is the last place you needed to conquer. What now?"

"There's always more," Lysli said. "There are stirrings in the east, beyond the mountains you call Malakai's Ridge. I must maintain control of my empire."

"To what end?" Ada asked. "You have everything you want, more than you could ever need. Do you only want to rule the world for the sake of ruling the world?"

"Oh, my dear simple peasant," Lysli laughed. "I want the one thing that has been denied every creature since time began. Eternal life."

51

"It seems you've already accomplished that," Ada said. "That is an ancient spell you're using. I've heard of it, but never seen it used. It was said in the last Age, the gods tried to use it to best one another."

"Indeed. And yet even they were killed or died off. I will be better than any of them. Stronger. I uncovered the secrets of this spell, and countless other spells used by the gods. I am as they, now. But even they were not infallible. I will be. That is why I have come here. This land holds ancient secrets, lost to time. The stories I've heard, the legends I've uncovered... I will be above the gods. I will have the power of the Creator."

She turned to look at Ada. "And you will help me."

Ada raised her chin. "If I do not?"

The cuff around her ankle began to burn, growing hotter by the second, sending tongues of flame up her ankle and through her body, searing her. Nausea churned in her stomach, growing ever more violent.

She gasped for breath, fighting to keep control of her body.

As quickly as it started, the pain faded, back down into the cuff around her ankle.

Lysli smiled, that smug, superior smile. "You will."

Ada bowed. "Yes, your Majesty."

She had to play along for now. Troy should be gone by now, and Sir Kire with him. He should be well on his way to the cairn. There...

She didn't know. It had been nearly a thousand years since the rest of her kind had gone into the cave. Were they dead? Had they laid eggs? Were they waiting for the end of this Age, when it was prophesied they would return? And what would happen when they did?

Lysli was powerful. She had the power of the gods of the last Age. Could she kill the dragons? Take their power for herself? Could she become as powerful as she wanted?

Ada didn't know, but nothing seemed outside the realm of possibility at this point. She had to prepare for the worst. And that meant being compliant. Staying alive long enough for Troy to succeed. Finding out Lysli's weaknesses. Creating a rebellion, turning against her, defeating her in the end.

They arrived at the queen's rooms, where the sorceress made herself at home entirely, establishing her sorcerer bodyguards in the adjoining servants' quarters and outside the door.

"You may go," Lysli said at last to Ada. "I presume you have a room of your own?"

Ada nodded.

"Go, then. Be back here at first light and we will discuss your role in my kingdom."

Ada made her way slowly down the long hallways to the stairs that descended to the lower level. She had no doubt Lysli would have her followed closely at all times from here on. Above all, she had to keep the amulet safe. As far as she knew, Lysli didn't know about the amulet or its power, and she hoped to keep it that way as long as possible. Still, though, her rooms would be searched. Any and all magical elements would be taken from her.

The safest place would be the Council room. But she couldn't risk drawing attention there. Not yet.

She detoured before she got to the staircase that led to her rooms and looked around. So far, no spies, that she could tell. She went to the kitchen. Empty at this hour. And truly, most of the servants would be hiding, waiting to find out what had happened and what would happen to them.

She passed through to the corridor on the other side, down the passages that led to cellars, and beyond, to the hidden door where the secret dungeons lay.

Down the long, narrow staircase, each step sending pain through her old, weary joints.

At last she came to the lowest level. The dungeon that had been built specifically to entrap those who could use magic. No magic could be sensed from inside—which meant Lysli wouldn't be able to sense the magic that emanated from the amulet from the outside.

Ada tucked the amulet into an old scrap of rags and set it in the corner of the cell third from the end, then made her way back up to the main levels, stopping for food in the kitchen along the way.

The next morning, she took Lysli on a tour of the castle, ending finally in the throne room. Lysli gathered up Queen Rina's sorcerers and put cuffs on them all, like the one she'd put on Ada. The Council members were hunted down and either killed or put in the dungeon—the regular one; Ada didn't tell Lysli about the other, magical one.

Within the day, seeing Ada and the other sorcerers as Lysli's slaves, the entire castle—and really, the entire kingdom—surrendered to Lysli.

The following morning, Lysli gathered Ada and the sorcerers—both hers and the Legerdemainians she had enslaved—on the parapet at the top of the castle.

She held a gem in her hand—a garnet, if Ada wasn't mistaken. Raising the garnet to the sky, she began to chant. Words in an ancient language. A language Ada hadn't heard in years, but knew the power of.

The language of the dragons.

"Hadima shalyi. Kal hakvich hiva shalyi."

The land is mine. All power is mine.

Magic streamed into the garnet, from all over the land. It drained from the sorcerers, from the trees, from the air, and settled into the garnet, for only Lysli to use.

A cloud formed from the garnet, the reaction of the earth to being drained of so much of its life force. The cloud rose into the sky, blotting out the sun and growing ever wider. With every bit of magic Lysli stole, the darkness spread.

The Journey

"Sir Kire!" Troy exhaled, feeling hope surge within him.

"Come. Time runs short." Sir Kire stepped around him and began to lead the way up the mountain.

"I thought you'd been killed by the monsters in the forest," Troy said.

"I almost was. One attacked me, shortly after your horse spooked. I was able to kill it. Another attacked. My horse ran, leaving me behind, but then the monster smelled the blood of the first and apparently decided that was better than chasing me. Easy meat."

"You're wounded," Troy said, noticing the older man's limp.

"I'll heal."

"Maybe you should rest. Maybe we…"

Sir Kire turned to glare at him. "Do you see that?" He gestured toward the dark cloud that hovered over the city below. "I don't know what it is, but I know it can't be good. There's no way the queen would allow something like that if she was alive. Nor Ada. We have to assume the worst. Our people are under the rule of the sorceress now, and we— *you*—are our only chance at rescue. Let's just hope your vision was the portent of something that will help."

Subdued, Troy followed Sir Kire ever higher up the slope. The trees thinned even more, until the two hiked beyond them completely. Open meadows of thin, yellow grass spread ever upward beyond them. But from here Troy could see the summit. They'd reach the top by nightfall.

They paused only briefly for food at midday, and by evening they had reached the top of the mountain. The cave was not here, however. There was no sign of the rock pillars or other signs that Troy had seen in his vision. More mountains lay beyond. It must be on one of those… but which one? How would he even know which way to go?

He turned to look back down at the valley below. The black cloud had covered the entire city and was spreading out to the fields. At this rate, in a day or two it would reach the villages. Then what? Would it spread beyond Legerdemain? How long until the whole earth was corrupted? Until crops stopped growing and animals died?

"I don't know which way to go," Troy told Sir Kire. "The vision didn't tell me. It could be in any direction, and I have no idea."

"We will rest," Sir Kire said. He gathered sticks and dried shrubs into a pile and built a fire. "In the morning, perhaps you can try to See."

"I can't. I've never been able to. I can't use magic the way my mother could. Or my father, apparently, if what the sorceress implied is true. He was the greatest sorcerer in the kingdom when he was alive, and yet I can't even do the simplest spells."

"Draw your sword," Sir Kire said.

Troy stared at him.

Sir Kire had already pulled his own sword out, capped the end with a piece of wood, and stood in a ready stance. "Come on."

Troy pulled his sword from its sheath. Walking had eased some of the tension in his muscles, but he was still sore, and it hurt to move.

Sir Kire lunged, and Troy shuffled back, parrying the strike.

Sir Kire twirled his wrist, sending the sword flashing in what seemed to be every direction at once, then lunged again, this time striking Troy in the chest with the blunted end.

"Watch my body, my eyes, but don't lose sight of my sword," Sir Kire said. "You must be aware of everything at once. What's the first rule?"

"Don't die," Troy said.

"Second?"

"Look for a weakness and exploit it."

"Exactly. If you keep on the defensive, your opponent will eventually make a mistake. That's when you strike."

Troy nodded and readied himself again, this time keeping his eyes the tip of the sword, while still being aware of Sir Kire's face and shoulders.

Sir Kire struck and Troy parried, again and again.

"Good," Sir Kire said, a small smile stretching is otherwise stoic features. "This time, when you get my sword out of the way, instead of retreating further, attack."

Troy obeyed. Sir Kire defended easily, but Troy kept going—defend, defend, defend, attack. It wasn't long before his arms tired and his sore muscles caught up to him.

"I need to rest," he said at last.

Sir Kire nodded and sheathed his sword. "Listen. When you're fighting, where is your focus?"

"On you... and on me. What you're doing, and how I can combat it."

"Exactly. Your mind is on both offense and defense. You must be aware of everything—the ground beneath you, your own body and movements, my body and my movements. You search for a weakness, an opening, and then you strike. It is the same with magic. Sit by the fire. Focus. Breathe. Be aware. Hear the animals, the crackling of the fire. Smell the smoke mingling with the fresh breeze. Notice everything. And then feel the magic. Look for that opening, and when you find it, strike."

Troy sat and stared into the fire. He watched the flames dance in the darkness. Felt the warmth ebb and flow as they caught the breeze. Listened to the crackling of the twigs, the wind in the trees, the night birds hooting, the small animals scurrying through the underbrush.

Focus on everything.

He closed his eyes and pictured the cave from his vision. Saw himself there, walking slowly between two of the pillars, toward the huge rock platform in the center. He looked up at the sky, judging the time of day. Midafternoon, if he wasn't mistaken. Turned around to get his bearings.

Mountains in every direction blocked his view of the valley of Legerdemain.

He couldn't see it.

But he could feel it. Something drew him back, some connection to his home tugging at his heart, giving him a sense of urgency and imminence. From where he stood at the top of the mountain, home was to the southwest.

He inhaled, grounding himself in the sensation of the mountaintop and the pillars and the stone slab that protected the cave. Feeling it. Knowing it. Finding it.

He opened his eyes.

Sir Kire stared at him, his gaze both penetrating and patient.

"I know where to go," Troy said.

A small smile touched Sir Kire's lips. "Let's get some rest, then. We have a long journey ahead of us."

Troy woke to the smell of meat sizzling over the fire.

Sir Kire stood by the fire roasting a rabbit.

They ate and refilled their water from a nearby stream.

"Well, your Highness? Which way?" Sir Kire asked.

Troy faced toward the northeast and closed his eyes. The pull toward the cave was as strong as the pull toward home. He didn't know if it was magic or the call of the vision, but he knew it was true.

"This way," he said.

They walked without stopping until past midday, down the other side of the mountain and up the next. After a quick meal, they began again and kept on up the mountain until it was nearly dark.

"This looks like as good a place as any to make camp," Sir Kire said at last.

They hadn't spoken much throughout the day. The walk was too strenuous.

Troy gathered wood and started a fire while Sir Kire hunted for fresh game. They ate, and then Sir Kire stood and drew his sword, capping the end with a piece of wood.

Troy sighed but pulled himself to his feet and stood in the ready stance.

His limbs almost refused to function, but he forced himself to defend against Sir Kire's relentless attacks. And once he had begun, he felt better. There was something soothing about going through the forms and letting his body react to what he knew that soothed him.

They stopped at last and Sir Kire clapped him on the back. "Well done. You improve more every day."

Troy's heart warmed. Sir Kire was not overly effusive with praise. A small compliment from him was worth more than a thousand from anyone else. "I have a good teacher," he said, not knowing what else to say.

Sir Kire grunted, but smiled.

"Get some rest," Sir Kire said. "We still have a long way to go."

Troy curled up in his blanket by the fire. "Sir Kire?"

"Yes?"

"Do you think they're all right?"

There was a long silence before Sir Kire answered.

"I think we need to get to that cave as quickly as possible and find whatever it is you were meant to find."

The Cellar

Lady Altya cowered in her room, listening as the sounds of the invading army tromped through the hallways.

She had almost no experience with a hostile takeover, save what she'd read in history books, but this seemed to be fairly peaceful. There wasn't violence happening outside, not unless someone resisted. Ada had ordered everyone to surrender peacefully, and for the most part, they were.

How could they not? The invading sorceress wielded the most powerful magic any of them had ever seen, and the army of sorcerers following in her wake did the same.

They hadn't come in here yet, but they would.

They were systematically searching the castle. Servants were given the option to serve the new queen—empress, rather—or be killed. A few had chosen death rather than serve the sorceress, and the others had to watch as the sorceress sucked the life from them, pulling their energy into herself, becoming more youthful and powerful even as her victims turned gray and their bodies withered and dried out.

Altya had watched from the shadows of the servants' hallways as the empress had gone through this process with the housekeeping staff. She'd run back up here to her room, not knowing where else to go.

But it was only a matter of time. They would find her. They would find out she was on the Council. She shouldn't even be on the Council.

She was too young. Scarcely older than the prince himself. She was an infant when Queen Rina took the throne. But her parents had been loyal to Rina. Her father died in the war against King William and her mother had been on the Council all these years.

When her mother had died two years ago, Queen Rina had asked Altya to join the Council herself.

Altya still didn't understand it fully. She had no magical ability, and very little political experience. But the queen trusted her.

Had trusted her. The queen was dead.

But what about Prince Troy? Was he still hiding in the Council room?

She considered going to him. But she couldn't risk drawing attention to his hiding spot. Ada had explicitly warned that no one was to go near him. No one but the Council and the posted guards knew where he was.

She should leave the palace. Hide in one of the villages. Maybe head south and leave Legerdemain entirely.

But Prince Troy was still alive, as far as she knew. And Ada was captured, enslaved to the sorceress. The rest of the Council—she had no idea. She hadn't seen any of the others since the sorceress arrived. Lady Brandys knew magic, so she would be enslaved like the others. Sir Kire… Sir Kire would probably be lurking somewhere, ready to protect the prince. If he hadn't died in the battle.

She should leave.

But the queen had trusted her. And she might be the only one left.

Yet what could she do? The queen was dead, the prince was hiding, and Ada, the most powerful sorceress in the kingdom, was a prisoner.

Perhaps if she left she could find help in Cadalania or Kirland.

But perhaps she would be of more use in the castle.

At any rate, she couldn't stay here cowering in her room. She would be found and taken prisoner, or worse.

Gathering a few items of personal value—her mother's wedding ring, her journal, and the necklace that her father had made for her when she was born, along with some extra clothes, she slipped out of her room and down to the servants' quarters.

"Lady Altya!" the head cook, Katte, gasped when she entered the kitchen. "We feared the worst. Where have you been?"

"Hiding," she admitted.

"Well done. We thought you'd been captured or killed. The sorceress has rounded up all the others and killed or enslaved them."

63

Altya's breath caught in her throat. "Then can we keep my not-death just between us?"

"Of course, dear. Come, this way." Katte led her to an empty storage room down the hall. "You can stay in here."

"For how long?" Altya asked.

"As long as it takes."

"No, I mean..." She took a deep breath, trying to find the words. "I can't just hide down here indefinitely. What if she finds Prince Troy? What if she kills him? Kills Ada? Even if I'm alive, but hiding, nothing will get better. I have to do something."

"Like what?"

"I don't know. I thought... maybe I should leave. Go to Cadalania or Kirland and try to get help. Or maybe be a spy here, and see if I can undermine her in some way."

Katte nodded slowly. "I know there are many who feel the same way. But they have no one to guide them. With the queen dead and Ada a prisoner, there is no one to take charge. But you... you are the last of the Council. They would follow you."

Altya's chin dropped and she shook her head. "I couldn't. I'm practically a child. No one would listen to me. But if I can get to Cadalania..."

Katte shook her head. "My dear, you underestimate yourself. You think the queen asked you to be on her Council because of your mother, but that's not true. She saw the wisdom and maturity in you in the way you handled your mother's death and estate, and in the wise counsel you give. Our people need a leader. We must fight this sorceress. And to do that, we need someone we can trust."

"I..." Altya stopped. She knew it was true. Not the part about being wise or mature, but the part about the people needing a leader in order to fight back against the sorceress. "I can't do it alone," she said at last.

"You won't have to," Katte said.

"I'll set up in here. This will be my sitting room, my office. I will need another place to sleep."

Katte walked toward the back of the storage room and opened a door into a small cellar. "There's just wine here now. We can move that out so you have a private space."

Altya walked down the few stone steps into the cellar. Once the barrels were removed, it would be plenty large enough for a sleeping space and a desk. And here, in the bowels of the castle, it would be unobtrusive. Servants would be expected to come in and out of the storage areas at all hours. It would be easy for those who joined her to come and go without notice, and it would be easy to stay hidden.

She turned to Katte. "This will do. No one must know I am here unless they have joined us. We can't risk anyone trying to curry favor with the empress by betraying me."

"Agreed," Katte said. "I will be very careful in vetting those who I allow to join us."

Within a matter of hours, Katte had helped Altya transform the cellar into a comfortable sleeping chamber and the storage room into a sitting room, complete with a desk and chairs, a cabinet for supplies, and parchment for writing and recording.

"I still think someone should go to Cadalania," Altya said when they were done. "I understand that I need to stay here and be the person organizing things, but someone should."

"I know some of the soldiers and even some of the stable hands had discussed leaving. I will ask around and see if I can find anyone who would be willing to go on a mission for you."

"Not for me," Altya corrected. "For us."

Katte smiled and inclined her head. "Of course."

The Tapestries

Ada knelt before Lysli in the throne room. Burning pain from the cuff around her ankle made her want to writhe on the ground, but she kept her position steady.

"You lied to me," Lysli said.

"I apologize, your Majesty." Her voice strained with the effort to keep it steady despite the pain. "What is it you think I lied about?"

"The boy," Lysli said.

"What boy?"

"The one who looks like Jarok. You told me he is nobody. But he is the prince. The queen's son."

Ada inhaled slowly. The sorceress was trying to trick her, to trap her into saying something by aggressive accusations. What was she trying to find out? Ada weighed her words carefully. "I never lied about that—I told you from the beginning who he was. I told you he has almost no magical ability, and that is true. I have attempted to train him myself, and he can do little more than grasp magical energy. He cannot even make a light."

"But he is the son of the queen, a woman who was renowned for her magical ability, and descended from one of the greatest sorcerers I have ever known. How is it possible he cannot use magic?"

"I do not know, Majesty. I myself was quite surprised at his lack of ability. Of course, I assumed it was because I thought his father was the queen's late husband, a soldier with no magical ability whatsoever, as far as I knew."

The pain in the cuff lessened slightly.

"The queen lied about who the boy's father was?"

Ada shrugged. "Or she did not know herself. But she always claimed it was her husband."

"Naturally. Well, I assure you, he is a descendant of Jarok. That much is clear just by looking at him. And Jarok's line was known for imbuing their offspring with extra magical abilities. Even this far removed, there should be some trace of it."

"Perhaps," Ada said. "But if so, I never figured out how to release it."

The cuff stopped burning and Ada drew in a deep breath to help her recover. She wished she could Heal it, but the cuff restricted her from using any magic that was not expressly permitted by Lysli.

"Never mind," Lysli said. "If there is magical ability in him, I will find it. Where is he now?"

Ada inhaled. She trusted that Troy had escaped as planned. It had been days—he had enough of a head start now that he would be hard to track, even if Lysli managed to find the secret tunnel. She just hoped Troy had the sense to return the tapestry to its place and close the door. But even if not, he was still outside the kingdom by now, and Lysli's army would have a hard time getting through the forest, past the monsters that still roamed there.

Still, though, it would not do for Lysli to think she was cooperating too easily.

So she remained silent.

The burn from the cuff started to crawl up her leg again.

"I told him to hide," she gasped at last.

"Where?" Lysli demanded.

"I will show you," Ada said.

Lysli stood from where she'd been seated on Rina's—or Troy's, now—throne and gestured for Ada to lead the way.

Ada hobbled down the long hallways and winding stairs toward the Council room.

The guards she'd posted outside the door straightened when they saw her coming, then stopped, fear painting their features when they saw Lysli followed by two of her sorcerer guards in their dark red robes.

"My lady…" one began.

Ada lifted a hand. "It's all right. She was going to find him eventually, anyway. I trust you have kept vigilant watch, and no one has been in or out?"

"No one, my lady. Not since the servant who brought him food and supplies left. The prince barred the door behind her, and no one has touched it from either side since."

"Good," Ada said.

She stepped forward and knocked on the door. "Your Highness, it's Ada. Open the door."

No one answered, and no sound came from the other side.

She pushed against the door, but it was barred from the inside.

Her pulse relaxed. Things seemed to have gone according to plan. She raised her voice, feigning worry, and pounded on the door again, a little louder this time.

"Your Highness. Troy! Please open the door!"

"Move," Lysli said.

Ada stepped out of the way and Lysli used magic to break the door in. She stepped inside and Ada followed her.

The room sat empty. No sign of Troy or any evidence that he had been in here at all.

Ada's eyes went to the tapestry behind which Troy would have escaped. It hung neatly, looking as though it hadn't been disturbed in hundreds of years.

Lysli turned in a slow circle, taking in every inch of the room. "How very curious. You said the boy has no magical ability?"

"Very little. So little it's almost imperceptible," Ada said.

"And yet he escaped from this room with no windows or doors." She turned to one of her sorcerers. "Take the guards to the dungeon and question them. Make sure they didn't let him escape."

Ada winced. She knew what their kind of questioning would involve. But she could do nothing for them. And it was better if she didn't—they knew nothing, and so they could tell nothing. Ada's intervention would only put them—and Troy—at greater risk.

"Find the servant, too. The one who brought him his supplies," Lysli said. She turned to Ada. "Where were you when he was locked in here?"

"I was with you. I left him here and came out to the wall. That was when you killed the queen and entered the city. I have been under your control ever since."

Lysli nodded slowly. "Very well. We shall see what the guards and servants know."

Ada tempered her reaction carefully. She could last longer under magical torture than the others, but if Lysli had even a hint that she knew more than she was saying, she wouldn't rest until she'd uncovered it.

Lysli turned again to look around the room. She waved at the tapestries hanging on the walls. "What are these?"

"They're tapestries, your Majesty."

A flare of pain in Ada's ankle reflected Lysli's irritation. "I know what they *are*. What I mean is, what are they pictures of? What do they mean?"

"They depict the history of our country," Ada said. She stepped forward and pointed at the picture of the one-armed man. "This was our first king, King Cerik. He was as wise as he was brave. He was asked to be king by the people. No one else even tried to contest the throne. His descendants have been on the throne ever since."

"And over the years, has no one ever tried to take the throne from his family?"

"Oh, they've tried. But King Cerik swore an oath that bound him and his family to this land for the rest of this Age. The magic that ties them to this land is stronger than any that anyone has been able to bring against them."

"Until me," Lysli said, a smug smile tugging the corners of her lips.

"Until you," Ada conceded.

Lysli walked slowly around the room, studying each tapestry in turn, until she reached the one with the dragons. She reached out to touch the image of the Elder, his purple scales shining in the sun.

"What are these?"

"Those are dragons. They were said to inhabit this land in the last Age. They gave over guardianship to the humans—to Cerik—to protect it in this Age."

A shudder visibly shook Lysli's body. The cuff around Ada's ankle grew cold.

Was it a premonition of some sort? Did Lysli See something?

Whatever the cause, it was clear Lysli feared the dragons.

Ada couldn't resist twisting that fear. "The prophecies say the dragons will return at the end of this Age and bring peace to the world. There are those who believe the omens to say that time is drawing near."

The Regent

"My lady, I have someone who would like to speak to you," Katte said, opening the door to Altya's storage room office.

"Enter," Altya said. She felt strange giving orders, but Katte insisted it was only right. Katte had become like a personal servant and secretary, despite still maintaining her role as head cook. She'd delegated some of those duties to others, but she could only do so much without inviting scrutiny and suspicion.

Katte stepped inside, leading a middle-aged gentleman who wrung his hat in his hands as he shuffled into the room and bowed.

Katte closed the door behind him. "This is Covah. He is a groomsman in the stables. His son was one of the soldiers killed in the empress's initial attack. He would like to help."

Altya looked up. "You're sure he can be trusted?"

"As sure as I can be about anyone," Katte said.

Altya looked at Covah, studying him. "You're a groomsman?"

He nodded.

"So you have access to the horses and no one would find it suspicious if you took one outside the castle?"

"They might find it suspicious, my lady, but I can do it."

"I need someone to leave the country and get to Cadalania. The empress has already been through there, so they must fear her. If you can, find someone who is willing to help raise an army against her. Preferably sorcerers. Can you do this?"

"I will do my utmost, my lady," Covah said. "Though I believe it will not be easy. Cadalania had few enough magic users to begin with. I imagine the empress would have enslaved any she found."

"Probably," Altya agreed. "But we must try. And if not magic users, then soldiers. And if not in Cadalania, then Kirland or Sunnland. However far you must go to get help. Anyone who wishes to overthrow her rule. Take one or two people with you, if you can find anyone you trust. Send me word if you can. I will do what I can here."

"Yes, my lady." Covah bowed again. Katte escorted him out, then returned a few minutes later.

Altya looked at the map she'd stolen from the library when she could sneak away. "By my figuring, if they make good time, they will be within Cadalania's borders in three days, then it will be another three or four to Winterborne. Within a fortnight we should receive word of some sort what is happening outside our borders and if they are likely to find help."

"Very good, my lady," Katte said. "What do we do in the meantime?"

"We have to assume the worst. What if there is no one to help us? What if Covah dies along the way? What if no one will come to our aid? What will we do then? If the worst happens, then we need to have a plan to defeat the empress on our own. We need an accurate count of just how many people she brought with her. How many soldiers, how many sorcerers? And how many of ours has she made her slaves? If she can control them, we cannot count them as being on our side until we free them."

"I will set our people to finding out and creating a comprehensive list, my lady."

Altya stood and paced the small room.

"I need to do something. Something more than hiding in this room all day every day. I need to..." She trailed off, unsure herself what she needed to do.

"What, my lady?" Katte said at last. "Get yourself captured? Killed? What then? Who would hold this kingdom together?"

Altya sighed. Katte was correct, of course, but it still burned to feel so useless.

The door to the storage room burst open and a man, one of the men who served in the throne room, Wystik, burst in. He was loyal—he'd been among the first to join their cause, and had been relaying every conversation he overheard, whether it seemed mundane or not, to Altya.

"My lady," he gasped. "It's... it's the prince."

Altya hurried to his side. "What about the prince? Has he been found? Is he captured? Killed?"

Wystik shook his head, still panting.

"No, my lady. He's... he's missing."

The shock of that statement settled over Altya. "Missing? What do you mean, *missing*?"

"The empress forced Ada to tell her where the prince was hidden and they went down to the Council room. The room has been locked and guards have been posted since before the empress took the city. No one has gone in or out. But when they opened the door, the prince was gone. No sign of him or where he went. He's just vanished."

Vanished.

This was not good news. How were they supposed to restore him to the throne if he was missing?

"You're sure he's not hiding somewhere else?"

"The empress is having the entire castle searched again, just in case, but she believes Ada told her the truth about the last time she saw the prince. And she had the guards tortured to make sure they weren't lying about letting him leave. He's just... gone."

What strange magic was this? Altya had never heard of a spell that could make someone disappear.

"I think... I think it is time for me to see some things for myself," she said. She turned to Katte. "Can you get me a servant's uniform? I will take the empress her tea."

Katte nodded and hurried from the room.

Altya took Wystik's hand. "Find out everything you can about what the guards told the empress. About what they know, and about what happened the night the empress took the castle. If the empress is looking for him, that means she didn't kill him. Although it's possible she's making a show of looking for him to cover up the fact that she killed him... No, that doesn't make sense. She would want us to know. She would use that to solidify her rule..."

She snapped her attention back to Wystik. "Just find out whatever you can and report back to me. And if you find others who are loyal to the prince, take them to Katte. No one must know who I am or what I'm doing unless absolutely necessary."

Wystik bowed. "As you say, my lady."

Katte returned and Altya dressed in the servants' clothes, then took the tea tray up to the throne room where the empress lounged on the queen's throne reading a scroll.

Altya set the tea tray down on a side table next to the throne.

"Taste it," the empress demanded without looking at her.

Altya paused. Was the empress speaking to her?

An old woman shuffled toward the table. Perhaps it was she who the empress was talking to.

Altya looked up as the woman reached for the cup of tea. She wasn't just any old woman. It was Ada.

Altya stifled a gasp.

The barest flicker of recognition twinkled in Ada's eye as she sipped the empress's tea and set the cup back down, then tasted one of the biscuits. Other than that, she gave no indication that she knew Altya was more than a servant.

"All seems to be in order, my lady," Ada said to the empress. "Not poisoned, so far as I can tell."

The empress nodded and reached for the biscuit, still not even looking at Altya.

"With your permission, I would like to go get something to eat," Ada said.

"Very well," the empress said, waving her away.

"Help me down, girl," Ada said, grasping Altya's arm.

Altya walked her down the dais steps and out into the hallway.

Once the door shut behind them, Ada turned and embraced her. "I feared you were killed," she whispered.

Altya smiled. "Not yet. I've been hiding in—"

"Don't tell me," Ada said. "It's better if I don't know. I'm just glad you're safe."

"For now," Altya said. "I just heard the prince is missing."

Ada nodded, her eyes narrowing slightly.

Altya gasped. "You know where he is."

"Not exactly," Ada said. "But I know he is alive, and I believe he will return. I just hope there's something for him to return to."

"That's what I'm trying to ensure," Altya said. "I'm working with any I can find who are loyal to him to undermine the empress's rule and save the kingdom for him."

"Then, by the authority given me under my oath and by the queen of Legerdemain, I name you regent until his return. Guard the kingdom well, for it is the only hope for the world."

The Canyon

Troy's legs burned. His empty stomach growled and his boots rubbed against raw blisters on his feet. How many mountains, now, had he and Sir Kire been up one side of and down the next? Each one seemed to be taller than the last, the terrain more rugged, the incline more steep, the resources more sparse. They hadn't passed a stream in two days, and their water skins only had drops left in them.

Game, too, had become more scarce, and even Sir Kire's hunting skills only produced results occasionally anymore. Troy glanced at his mentor. He couldn't begin to express his gratefulness. Not just for the hunting and experience he offered, but for the company. Troy would've died days ago if it hadn't been for Sir Kire. More, he would've lost hope.

Every night, Troy tried to feel—or See, or whatever it was he was doing—and he still felt sure they were going the right direction, but it was getting harder to have confidence they'd ever make it to their destination the longer this trek continued.

And every day, the black cloud that covered Legerdemain seemed to grow larger. It had not yet reached them, but from the tops of the peaks he could see it had already started to cover the first mountain and snake around behind it into the valley on the other side.

The sun cast long shadows as it sank toward the mountains to the west. They needed to find a place to camp. But they also needed to keep moving. But they couldn't keep moving without water and food. Which meant they needed to hurry to find their destination before they had no resources left.

"It looks like there's an overhang under that cliff," Sir Kire said, nodding toward the peak ahead of them. "That will be a good place to rest."

Troy nodded, too tired to talk.

They reached the overhang just before dusk and Sir Kire built a small fire using brush and dried grasses he scavenged from the ground. This high, even in summer, the wind cut like an icy knife through their cloaks and blankets.

They nibbled at the little bit of food they had left and sipped at the few drops of remaining water.

Sir Kire stood. "Draw your sword."

Troy groaned but obeyed. Their training sessions had gotten shorter every night, but Sir Kire insisted on maintaining the discipline of the routine.

Truthfully, Troy appreciated it. The continuance of routine, however small, kept them both sane.

"Begin," Sir Kire said.

Troy parried as well as he could, but as tired and worn as he was, he couldn't even keep his arms up for very long.

Time after time, Sir Kire jabbed him.

"That's enough for tonight," Sir Kire said after a couple rounds. "Remember, it's not about strength as much as speed and control. Don't let your guard down."

Troy nodded, but it was so hard to think. So hard to focus on anything when everything hurt.

Sir Kire sighed as he settled in beside the fire. "In the morning, we will need to look for water before we continue on our way. Where there is water, there will also be game."

Troy just hoped that they could find something before they both died. He curled up into a ball beneath his blanket.

They woke late. The sun didn't reach them until mid-morning. But not because of the overhang.

The blackness in the sky had stretched over the horizon so it blocked even the sun for the first few hours of the day.

Sir Kire stared at the cloud for a long time before turning to Troy. "Our time is running short. The sorceress gains more power every moment. That—" he waved toward the cloud—"That does not bode well. I just hope it is not already too late."

A stone seemed to settle in Troy's stomach.

He trudged upward toward the next peak, hoping to find what he was looking for on the other side. Not long now—they'd be to the top of this mountain by midafternoon.

The sun felt cold, and a strange mix of heat from exertion and chill from the wind snapped him back and forth, never settling to a comfortable temperature. Not that the temperature was his primary concern, but it made it that much more difficult to press on.

They approached a ridge. This was the highest mountain yet, and he couldn't see the peaks of any beyond, so perhaps they'd soon be reaching the other side of this range.

Sir Kire stepped out ahead, pulling himself up on a rock, then another, climbing up a steep face.

Troy heaved a deep breath and followed him up. He was almost to the top when Sir Kire yelped, his voice morphing to a yell of terror, then cutting off completely.

"Sir Kire!" Troy yelled. He scrambled the last few feet to the top of the ridge. The other side fell away in a sheer cliff. He stepped backwards, almost falling back the way he'd come, before he found his balance.

He stared down the side of the cliff, but saw no sign of Sir Kire other than the crumbling shale at the top where Sir Kire's foot had slipped. The bottom of the canyon lay far below, covered in mist. Far to the other side, another cliff rose up.

A large bird swooped out from somewhere on the cliff below and circled above the chasm.

Sir Kire was gone.

He stared for a long time, as the weight of that reality settled down on him. Sir Kire was dead. He was alone. And trapped on the top of this mountain with no way to get down or across.

For a brief moment, he considered jumping. Joining Sir Kire at the bottom of the gorge. Letting his mother and whoever was left in Legerdemain fend for themselves.

But his mother needed him. The kingdom needed him.

He couldn't let them down. Not on purpose, anyway.

He scanned the ridge to either side. He could go back down, try to find a way around. But that would take even more time. And he still had no food or water.

But he couldn't go straight down. There was no path and the cliff face was much too steep.

Left—west—would take him further away from his destination, which he felt was still to the northeast. The ridge he stood on sloped away gently to his right, following the edge of the canyon.

That was his only option. He would follow that as far as he could and hope he eventually found a place where he could go down into the canyon safely.

He trekked along the ridge, edging his way down the side he'd come up just a little so if he fell he didn't tumble completely into the canyon.

The ridge never seemed to end. It sloped slowly downward, but there was not a game trail or any sign of the cliff face becoming less sheer.

Darkness would be upon him soon, and there was no place to camp. Every step was precarious. Even down the way he'd come was steep and treacherous. He couldn't very well sleep on the ridge, and he couldn't walk in the dark.

The cloud of darkness from Legerdemain stretched toward him. By morning he might have no light at all. He had to find a way into the valley before nightfall.

He trudged a little faster, scanning the ridge ahead for any sign of relief.

Another hour, and the path was so dim he could scarcely see one step in front of him. He stepped carefully, trying not to veer too far to one side or the other.

Perhaps he could find a small nook to nestle into, and sit through the night.

He reached out with one toe, feeling for the next sure step, and set his foot down.

It slid on a loose rock, sending his weight off-balance, and his body launching forward and to the side.

The cliff side.

He reached out with his hands and scrabbled for any hold as he slid.

Rocks scratched his hands and arms as he sought purchase, but there was nothing. He bounced from a ledge and rolled, smacking against another slight ledge and another as he tumbled down, over and over, until his head smacked against something hard and he knew no more.

81

The Seeing

"You will tell me everything there is to know about the magic in this land," Lysli said. "And the prophecies."

Ada led Lysli to the library, where books and scrolls lined the shelves. She pulled down a scroll and unrolled it on the long, wooden table. "This was written by a scribe during King Cerik's reign," she said. "It tells of the journey King Cerik took from his land to Legerdemain. The monsters they faced, and how they defeated the gods to claim this land."

The scroll had a sister, one Ada was not planning to share with Lysli. The one that told about the dragons and the Trials.

The one that would reveal Ada's true identity.

"The dragons lived here at that time," Ada said. "They were magical creatures, like the gods, but they did not wish for power. They remained here while the Great War raged in the rest of the world. When Cerik and his people came, they knew it was their time to go and leave this land for the Age of Men."

"Where did they go?" Lysli asked.

"Nobody knows. The mountains, it is believed. The old folklore suggests that the gemstones that were mined from the mountains, for which Legerdemain was famous, were the bodies of dragons who died."

"Even in Oajure we'd heard of Legerdemainian gemstones," Lysli said. "It cost a high price to import them. But the best sorcerers had them and swore they were better for channeling magic than other gemstones. I had a few, but I could never tell a difference."

She snapped her attention back to the scroll. "How did Cerik become bound to the land? How does the magic work, that it made him stronger than any other?"

"No one knows for sure. The dragons made him swear an oath, using a spell that has been lost to time. He swore using his own magic, mixed with the magic of the dragons, that he and his line would protect this land throughout the Age."

"How? What did they do to make the oath binding?"

"There was a potion—mixed by one of the dragons—and a gemstone, and magic. Possibly blood. And an incantation."

"Yes, that makes sense," Lysli said, more to herself than to Ada. "In my travels, I have discovered different types of magic are used by different people. In Oajure, we use primarily gemstones and incantations in the ancient language. Until Reith came, I didn't even know magic could be drawn from plants. We knew nothing of potions. The Barbarians on the continent south of yours use potions almost exclusively."

Lysli toyed with the garnet on the ring she wore. "In the Amarinian empire, they use language almost exclusively. They have a little knowledge of herbs, but they have almost no gemstones. I learned many new incantations while I was there."

"You really have traveled the world," Ada breathed.

In all her years, Ada had hardly ventured outside Legerdemain. A thing she should have done, except there was always something happening at home that needed her attention.

Perhaps, if she lived through this Age…

Not a scenario she could count on. Her purpose was here. And right now, that meant helping this witch learn new magic.

"Tell me about the prophecy," Lysli said. "I keep overhearing rumors about it. People seem to think my coming is a portent of the end of this Age."

Ada weighed her options carefully. Lysli would find out eventually. And she still had to cooperate. As long as she was a prisoner—and as long as Troy was gone and safe—she could not afford for Lysli to be angry with her. Lysli might not be able to kill her using her magic- and life-sucking spell, but that didn't mean she couldn't find another way. Or just imprison her. Ada would be useless to Troy and to Legerdemain if she was locked away.

She needed to stay close to Lysli if she was going to be of any help.

So she walked slowly to the shelves and pulled down an old scroll. Not the original, but a copy that had been around almost as long.

She spread the scroll before Lysli. "These are the words of the prophecy spoken by King Cerik in the first age."

Lysli examined the scroll. "Which part do the people think pertains to me?"

Ada pointed to a stanza near the bottom of the prophecy. "When the darkness reigns, then the hate shall bind the hearts of one and all until the light is found."

"Interesting. Because of the cloud?"

Ada nodded.

"That will dissipate in a few weeks. It's nothing to worry about."

"As you say, your Majesty."

"What does this mean?"

Ada leaned over to see the phrase she pointed to.

"What is the dragon stone?" Lysli asked.

"I'm afraid I cannot answer that."

"Can't or won't?" Lysli asked.

Ada sighed, hoping she sounded condescending enough to express her disdain at the question, but not so much that Lysli would feel the need to punish her. "No one knows for sure what the dragon stone is. That's the thing about prophecy. Most of the time you don't know until after the fact what it really meant. For example, I don't believe all of these things are yet to come. I think some of the prophecy has already been fulfilled."

She found the stanza she sought and pointed to it. "*Across the ocean wide, the darkness rises swiftly. Untold power unleashed, building until that day.* I believe that references Reith."

"And thus also me," Lysli said.

"Perhaps. But also perhaps Jarok. He unleashed much darkness when he was here."

Lysli stood abruptly and shoved the scroll away. "There is nothing more for me to learn from this. At least not now. I have learned magic from all over the world, and yet one thing eludes me, one thing that I have only ever heard of from here. You will show me how to See."

84

Ada's throat clenched.

Seeing was powerful. If Lysli could See, it might make her more dangerous. And yet… the future could not be changed. And Seeing was an art. Unlike other forms of magic, there were no guarantees with Seeing.

There was a chance Lysli wouldn't be able to do it at all. And yet if she did—what would happen, what kinds of tortures might she rain down if she didn't like what she Saw?

Ada hated the thought of teaching such a powerful thing to someone so without conscience. Yet, what choice did she have?

"Very well. If you will allow me to gather some supplies, I will meet you in your chambers."

A short while later, Ada assembled her collection of herbs and a bowl of water on the table in Lysli's room.

She looked at Lysli and said the same thing she'd said to every student she'd taught to See. "Seeing is a window into another time or place. The future cannot be changed. What you See is what will be. But sometimes, what you See is not what you think."

"But if I can See it, then I can prepare for it."

"Perhaps," Ada said. "But just because you See it doesn't mean it will happen the way you think it will. And sometimes, in trying to avoid the fate you See, you cause it to come to be. Also, as it is a window, it doesn't always work. And if it does, you may not See what you are hoping."

"Enough. Just show me how it is done."

Ada nodded and prayed that her actions would not bring more harm to Legerdemain.

The World

"There's been another murder, my lady," Katte said.

Altya sighed. "Who this time?"

"One of the upstairs servants. She was last seen serving the empress's sorceress slaves. Her body was found in the servant's hallway on the second level. The rumors say she was feeding information to the sorceress about who is and is not loyal, and she was killed by one of those who wanted to rebel."

"We have to stop killing each other. This will never work if we suspect everyone."

"I know, my lady," Katte said. "But the people are afraid. They don't know who to trust. And so far there are very few I trust enough to bring into our fold. Any one of them could betray you to curry favor with the empress."

"Perhaps there is something we can do to give them hope. Perhaps if they know we exist—even if they don't know who or where we are—it will help to encourage them to get along."

"Or it will make them more suspicious of one another," Katte said. "Besides, what can we give them hope with? The prince is still missing. No one knows if he's alive or dead. Ada looks like she's getting older and weaker by the minute. She cannot save us. And every day the darkness grows. Crops are failing and animals are dying."

She was right.

There was no hope.

But perhaps, if they could kill the empress…

That was a plot that would take some doing. It had been tried. One of Queen Rina's guards, a merchant, and a couple servants had all attempted it. The guard was killed by magic the moment he rose his hand to strike. One of the servants had attempted poisoning her food, but had nearly killed Ada who was given the task of food tasting. And the other servant had attempted to smother her in her sleep, but one of the sorceress slaves had stopped her. She'd been interrogated and put to death a day later.

But Altya couldn't give up.

She wouldn't.

She dismissed Katte and went over her notes on the schedules of the servants and guards. The empress spent most of her day in the library with Ada. Learning… what? She didn't seem interested in the history of the kingdom, and certainly not in its future. All she wanted was more power.

And she was getting it, more than she realized. True power was utter control, and she had so much control that no one even cared to live anymore. Anger and jealousy and bitterness erupted every day. Half the palace staff had committed suicide. Others had killed family members in an attempt to save them from the agony of this life. Still others had attempted to flee, only to be killed by the empress's sorcerers.

Some must have made it out of the kingdom alive. They *must* have.

A heavy knock at the door jolted her from her thoughts.

"Enter," she said.

Katte burst in almost before she'd finished speaking, breathless, leading a man behind her.

"Covah," Altya gasped. "You're back."

Covah stumbled in and fell into a chair opposite Altya's desk. Several days' growth of stubble adorned his chin, and the circles under his eyes suggested he hadn't slept in days.

"Get him food and drink," Altya said to Katte.

Katte hurried to obey and Altya leaned forward and rested her elbows on her desk. "What did you find out? Is Cadalania willing to help us?"

Covah shook his head. "There is no one. Anywhere."

Fear gripped Altya's chest. "What do you mean?"

"The darkness is everywhere. I went all through Cadalania, down even to Sunnland, then up the coast to Kirland. People still live, in suspicious and violent clusters. The food is almost gone. There are the bodies of the dead—those that haven't been picked clean by scavengers—everywhere. The entire land smells of death. Even the sea is covered in darkness, and the bodies of the fish and other creatures that have died are washed up on the shore. The few people I could get to even talk to me had no interest in joining us or helping us defeat the sorceress. We are alone, and it's only a matter of time until we end up like them."

Altya's heart sank.

How was this possible? How could the sorceress have destroyed everything so quickly, and without them hearing any news of it?

And how could they hope to defeat her when she had already overtaken the entire world?

Eventually, when everything was destroyed, she would die too. She got her power by draining it from others, and if there was no one left, she would eventually die the queen of nothing. Or she'd starve to death, when the food supplies ran out. But by then everyone else would be dead, too.

What was she hoping to rule, when she'd killed everyone? How was she planning to be the empress of the world if everyone was dead?

Or perhaps she didn't know. Perhaps she didn't realize just what her magic had done. Perhaps she thought things would settle back to normal after she left. Perhaps…

Altya sighed. Somehow, she needed to make the empress understand. Somehow, she needed to tell her that Legerdemain would end up like the rest of the continent if she continued as she was, sucking all the power out of everyone and everything. Surely she couldn't desire to be the queen of death and nothingness. What good was it to have power if you destroyed everyone and everything?

But the sorceress had no reason to listen to Altya. No reason to believe her or care what Altya's information said. She did not have any motivation to trust Altya's counsel on this. And if she did find out Altya's role, rather than listening, the sorceress would probably just kill her.

The only one who might have the slightest chance of getting through to her was Ada. The one person the sorceress hadn't yet been able to conquer. The one person who might still have power, despite her scheming.

"Get me a servant's uniform," Altya said to Katte. "I need to go see Ada.

"My lady, are you sure that's wise?"

"We are past the point when wisdom would be useful. This is urgent."

"And if you are caught?"

"Then I will die trying to save this land."

Katte sighed, but nodded. She led Covah from the room and returned a few minutes later with a uniform.

Altya dressed, then took a tray of food—already the food stores were growing thin and wilted—and made her way up to the throne room where Ada stood dutifully next to the sorceress.

Ada's eyes widened slightly as she registered who it was who brought the food.

Altya tried to convey with her eyes the urgency of her visit, and Ada nodded, almost imperceptibly.

Altya made her way slowly out of the room.

Behind her, Ada tested the food, then said to the empress, "Please excuse me for a moment. I must relieve myself."

As she left the throne room, from the corner of her eye, Altya saw the empress wave Ada off dismissively.

Altya waited in a servant's alcove for Ada to emerge.

Ada met her and together they walked through a servant's corridor until they were out of sight and hearing from anyone who might pass by.

"What is it?" Ada asked.

Altya took a deep breath, not sure how to explain what Covah had seen. At last, all she could think to say was, "The world really is ending."

The Ultimatum

Ada bowed before Lysli.

She'd waited a full day so no suspicion would fall on Altya before approaching the sorceress with her information.

"I have heard news," Ada said.

"Oh? And where did you hear it from?" Lysli asked.

"A refugee."

"There are no refugees."

"Indeed. This as an anomaly. I received the message from someone in one of the villages who met the refugee by the river. Do you know why there are no refugees?"

Lysli's eyes narrowed. "Tell me your opinion." She said the words as though anything Ada said would be suspect, as though she didn't believe Ada's information could possibly be valid, but she was willing to humor her.

"The world is dead. The sun has not returned. Every country is black as this one. Plants and people are dead and dying, and there is no recovering. You have destroyed everyone, and you will soon destroy us. Who will you rule when everyone is dead but you? How will you continue to live when everyone from whom you could steal life is gone?"

Lysli slammed her hand down on the arm of the throne. "This is your doing! I came here for help. You're not dead! All I wanted was to know how you did it—how you lived so long. How you cheated death. I don't want everyone to die, I just want to live."

"Everyone dies," Ada spat.

"You don't!" Lysli screamed.

This was the first time Ada had seen her lose her cool demeanor and detached control.

She decided to press her advantage. "You are a fool. You've been alive for hundreds of years and you are still no more mature than a toddler."

"I am a goddess!"

"You are the goddess of nothing."

All at once, Lysli regained her self-control. "But I will be goddess of everything. You have the power of the gods. You have been alive for longer than I, without destroying your land or your people. Indeed, this land is rich with magic, more potent than any I have ever felt. This land thrives, and you with it. You will show me how, or eventually I will weaken you enough that I can take your power, and when your power is mine, I will be like you, and I will heal the land."

Ada sighed and allowed her disdain to creep into her voice. "You understand nothing. My longevity is not my power, it is my weakness. I did not get it by taking, but by giving. I sacrificed any chance I had at living for myself—any opportunities for home or wealth or even love—to this country. I made a vow, and the magic that binds me to my vow binds me to this land. I will live as long as it needs to be protected."

She looked Lysli up and down. "You are right about one thing. You will eventually weaken me enough to kill me. When you succeed in destroying this land and everyone in it, then I will have failed in my duty and I will die. But my power will not be yours, and you will still be the goddess of nothing but death."

"Tell me about this vow," Lysli said, sitting up straighter. "How does it work? What did you do?"

Ada sighed. Lysli hadn't heard a word she said. "I don't know," she said. "There was a potion, but I don't know what was in it. And blood. And an artifact made from the pieces of talismans of the gods and a gemstone."

"If I gather these things, I can make the same vow."

"No, you can't," Ada said. "The ritual was performed by the former inhabitants of this land. They passed their guardianship from themselves to the first king, and I volunteered to be his protector."

"So the ritual must performed by the ruler of the land." A devious smile twisted Lysli's lips. "Young Jarok. The prince you claimed was powerless. It seems he is useful to me after all."

"That's not what I said," Ada tried to tell her, but she wasn't listening.

Lysli stood and swept from the room, hollering at whomever would listen that they were to gather everyone—every villager, every soldier, every servant—and meet in the courtyard the following morning.

Morning came, though it was hardly distinguishable from night. Ada followed Lysli out onto the platform that skirted one edge of the courtyard. Torches were lit all around, but still the fog of Lysli's darkness encroached, making everything seem muted.

Lysli used magic to bolster the flames in the torches, but it was only marginally successful.

Despite that, however, the courtyard was filled with haggard people, desperate for any news, any sign of change, anything that might give them enough hope to hold on for another day.

Using another spell to amplify her voice, Lysli addressed the people.

"The prince is missing. This blackness, this death that is all around—I can fix it, but I need the prince. He is the key to fixing this land. I have stores of food in the castle. Whoever finds the prince and returns him to me will have all their family can use until the land is restored and they can continue to provide for themselves."

Ada tried to interject, to tell the people her words were lies, but the moment she opened her mouth, the cuff around her ankle burned and her voice was stifled.

Lysli glanced at her, a snide smirk on her face, as if to say Ada should know better than to even attempt it.

Not for the first time, Ada considered how to remove the cuff. It was controlled by magic. Specifically by Lysli. But it was also automatic, as though the spell was woven into the cuff itself. There must be a way to break it. But she couldn't use magic to explore the spell or the cuff, and everyone else with any magical ability was either dead or also cuffed.

If only she could get word to the prince. But it was too dangerous to even try. She knew where he had gone, but she couldn't risk sending anyone after him. The potential for betrayal or capture was too great.

The people were desperate, and they would do whatever they thought would help them in this darkness.

The prince would return. And he would bring help.

She had to believe that. She couldn't See it. Even before she was cuffed, the future was blank. Unwritten. The things that were Seen would always come to pass, but the outcome of this... all she knew was the world would either live or die based on the war that would come. And Lysli and Troy were the two forces that would battle and ultimately either break it or heal it.

Lysli went on and on, about her plans for a bright and prosperous future, not just for Legerdemain but for the world, and how soon she would be able to give them everything they desired. Her magic was strong, but she needed the prince. Anyone who kept the prince hidden or helped him to escape was guilty of dooming the rest of them.

Ada sighed.

Lysli's words would only make things worse. So much worse. Neighbors would become suspicious of one another, even more so than they were now, each wondering if the next was the one who had doomed them all by hiding Prince Troy, all fighting against one another to receive the reward Lysli promised and to survive another day.

At last, Lysli finished her speech and turned to go back inside. Once the doors shut behind her, she turned to Ada. "I will live forever. Even if you hide your secret, I will find another secret, or another after that. If you tell me, then I will use that power to make the world better for everyone. But if you do not, I will just kill you. It is your choice whether you wish to die on your stubbornness or whether you will die to save these people you claim to care so much about."

Lysli turned and stalked away.

There was nothing Ada could do until Troy returned.

Ada could not go herself—Lysli watched her too closely—but perhaps she could send someone else into the tunnel to keep watch. That was where Troy would come when he returned, and she wanted to make sure he could get back safely.

When he returned... then they could begin to make things right.

The Freed

Katte knocked on the door but didn't wait for Altya to respond before entering.

Altya looked up and smiled as welcomingly as she could despite the raging headache that threatened to cripple her.

"Come in," she said. "What is it?"

A woman followed Katte into the room. A woman with a cuff around her ankle.

"This is Maryn," Katte said.

Panic shot through Altya, intensifying her headache. "Why did you bring her? The empress will know where she has been—she'll force her to tell—she'll—"

"My lady, if I may explain," the sorceress said softly.

Altya took a deep breath and nodded.

"I have been studying how the cuffs work," Maryn said. "They are put in place and controlled by magic—but the magic is external. It's not actually linked to me. If I can get the cuff off, then I will be free. The problem is, it can only be controlled by magic, and as long as I'm wearing it, I cannot use magic without express permission from the empress. That means I cannot remove it from myself or any of the others."

"I understand," Altya said. "But I don't understand how I can help. I can't use magic, and everyone who can is also wearing a cuff."

"Yes," Maryn said. "The cuff cannot be cut off, and any damage to it results in alerting the empress, as well as causing me debilitating pain. I also cannot harm myself. I have attempted suicide several times, but the pain makes it so I cannot follow through on any of my plans. But I believe I have found a solution."

Altya raised an eyebrow. "What is that?"

"You must cut off my foot."

Altya gasped and Katte gulped loud enough for it to echo in the tiny room.

"You can't be serious," Altya said after a few moments. "You'll be permanently crippled."

"I know," Maryn said. "I would rather be without a foot than forced to use magic to further the empress's agenda or die feeding her power. I cannot do it myself. I've tried. You must."

Altya stared at her for a long time. "If you are free, you can use magic."

Maryn nodded.

"And you know how the cuffs work? Can you remove them from the others?"

"I don't know," Maryn said. "I can try."

Altya considered the ramifications of this. It was a sacrifice she would never ask anyone to make. But Maryn volunteered. And they needed this. They needed to have an advantage. "Very well. Katte, do you have something that will numb the pain?"

"I can make a potion," Maryn said. "It will make me sleep, and it will numb the pain after I wake up. The mixing of the potion doesn't actually require magic. I just need the right supplies."

"Very well. Katte, help her get what she needs. Make the potion. Katte, do we have a butcher or blacksmith with the tools to make a clean cut?"

"I will find someone, my lady," Katte said.

"Do it quickly," Altya said. "We can't have the empress coming down here looking for her, wondering why she has been gone so long."

"Right away, my lady."

Within a few minutes, Maryn had her potion ready and Katte had found the butcher and his giant cleaver.

95

The butcher heated his cleaver in the fire until it burned red-hot. "To cauterize the wound so she doesn't bleed to death," he told Altya.

Altya nodded. "Are you ready?" she asked Maryn.

Maryn gulped, but nodded. She sat on the floor by the hearth, leaning up against Katte for support. Altya sat on the floor next to her and held her leg, bound in a towel.

"Let's get this done." Maryn gulped down her potion. Within moments, her head lolled in Katte's lap, her eyes fluttering closed.

Altya took a deep breath and nodded at the butcher.

He also paused, as though mentally preparing himself for the task he was about to perform. He drew the cleaver from the flames, steadied it just below the cuff, then drew it back and chopped down in one fluid motion.

Maryn groaned and flopped around as Katte tried to hold her still so Altya could pull the cuff from her leg and bind the wound. The cut was clean, and the heat from the blade had been mostly successful in cauterizing it so it wasn't gushing blood, but it would need care.

And Maryn would need lots of rest.

"Help me carry her," Altya ordered.

The butcher lifted her easily and cradled her in his arms. "Where do you want me to take her?"

"This way," Altya said. She led the way down the hallway to a storage room that was now empty, the food having been used up in the famine that had resulted from the empress's darkness.

When they had made Maryn as comfortable as possible on a mat on the floor, Altya went back to the nearly empty kitchen.

Maryn's foot still lay on the floor by the fire, untouched by any of the servants. The cuff sat next to it, stained with blood, but intact.

Altya wrapped the foot carefully in a rag and placed it in a burlap bag, then did the same with the cuff, in a different bag. She hid the cuff in a corner of a store room that still had some rice and beans and other foods, tucked away where it should go unnoticed.

She assigned Katte to care for Maryn, then took Maryn's foot outside. The garden was empty—everything was empty, really. People huddled indoors, just trying to stay alive as long as possible, and there was no one to see her bury the foot at the base of a tree.

She just hoped it was worth it.

She returned to the kitchen and started to walk toward her office when a bellow echoed down the hall. The empress.

She ducked into an alcove to hide as the empress stormed into the room.

"Where is she?" the empress demanded.

"Where is who, my lady?" one of the cooks asked.

Altya kept hidden, leaning out of her alcove just enough to watch what the empress would do.

"My slave," the empress growled. "I felt her cuff come off, which is impossible. Where is she? How did she do it?"

The cook glanced at another, then turned back to the empress. "She's dead, my lady. She came in here to ask for something to eat. I handed her a loaf of bread, and she asked for a knife. I saw no reason not to give it to her. But instead of cutting the bread, she plunged it into her chest."

"That's not possible! She can't willfully harm herself."

The cook shrugged. "I cannot explain how, your majesty, I only can tell you what I saw."

"Where is her body?" the empress demanded.

"We asked two of the soldiers to take her out. I believe they were going to take her beyond the city gates to bury her."

The empress screamed again and stretched her hand toward the cook. The cook gasped and her skin shriveled up, and a moment later her dried-out body collapsed to the floor.

The second cook turned and tried to run, but she wasn't fast enough. The empress did the same to her, sucking out her life and leaving her a husk on the floor.

As soon as the empress left the kitchen, Altya snuck back to her office. A few hours later, Katte knocked on the door.

"Maryn is awake. She Healed her wound as best as she could—apparently it is very difficult to Heal oneself, but she was able to Heal it enough that it should heal the rest of the way on its own without causing her too much pain."

"Good. Thank you."

"She... she wishes to have the cuff. To study it. To see if she will be able to figure out how it works, and free some of the others."

Altya retrieved the cuff and took it to the room where Maryn sat, her leg still bound.

For days, she returned periodically and watched as Maryn held the cuff, turning it over and over in her hands.

The fourth day, she sat down to try to help. There was nothing much she could do anyway, with all her people dying at the hands of the empress.

"Any luck?" she asked.

Maryn shrugged. "I can feel the various components. I think I'm making progress in unraveling them."

Maryn closed her eyes, and remained that way for so long, Altya wondered if she'd fallen asleep. She was about to sneak out and leave Maryn to rest, when a sort of cracking sound echoed through the small store room and the cuff snapped open.

Maryn's eyes bulged and a grin spread across her face.

"I did it! I figured it out! It's very clever—the spell that makes it work is like a braid, or a series of knots, that must be unwoven very carefully. But now that I know what I'm doing, I should be able to do it on the others.

"I will send someone to begin getting the magic users down here."

"Slowly," Maryn warned. "You know what happened when she thought I died. We cannot have her killing everyone in sight if she figures out what we're doing. One at a time, spread out over days."

Altya nodded. More would die. Every day, there were those who had given up, losing the will to live and dying on their own. But now they had a way to fight back.

The Cairn

Troy woke to a shaft of sunlight blinding his eyes. Just one thin shaft, sneaking between the edge of the cliff above and the billowing darkness overhead, but it was enough to make him close his eyes again.

He ached all over. He couldn't even tell where one ache stopped and the next began. His skin, his muscles, his head—especially his head—everything throbbed.

He blinked against the sun and tried to roll over.

His body refused to obey.

He closed his eyes and lay still, breathing as deeply as his sore body would allow, trying to summon the energy to move. Perhaps he shouldn't. Perhaps it wasn't worth it. Someone else could stop the sorceress. Ada would find a way. She must.

He couldn't go on. He'd done his best. His mother would be proud of how hard he'd tried. Sir Kire would be proud. Even Ada would be, if she knew. He'd done all he could, and now... now he was done.

The inside of his mouth felt thick, his tongue coated with what felt like a dry paste.

The sun moved—or maybe it was the black cloud—and his eyes were no longer being burned by the light.

A sound registered in the back of his mind, growing clearer as he focused on it. A steady rumbling. He knew that sound.

Running water.

There was a stream nearby.

His thirst stabbed at him, urging him to find the water. The innate will to survive battled with his exhaustion. He wanted to give up. How long would it take to die if he didn't move at all? Would his body go numb from the pain, or would he lie here in agony for hours or even days first?

The sky darkened further. Through the pain, something called to him. Far to the south, the heartbeat of Legerdemain reached out to him, begging.

His mother couldn't save them. Ada couldn't. If any of them were even still alive. No one could fix this.

He was the only one left, and if he died here in this canyon, everyone else would die, too.

He took a deep breath and rolled slowly over onto his stomach, his body aching with every inch. Pain stabbed through him at a thousand points. He paused to breathe. Even breathing was painful.

Three breaths. He would take three breaths, and then he would move.

One... Two... Three.

He reached one arm in front of him and pulled on the rocky dirt, pushing with his legs to inch forward. The other arm forward, pull. Now push with his legs. One after the other, stopping every few inches to rest and breathe, heading toward the sound of water.

What seemed like hours later, the ground began to feel softer. More plant life grew here. He was getting close. That also made it easier to crawl, with grass and moss beneath him instead of dirt and rocks.

Arm, legs, other arm, legs, breathe. Over and over.

And then there it was. The stream, tumbling over rocks in a steady rhythm. He pulled himself the last few inches and stuck his sweaty head into the stream, submerging it in the icy water. He lapped up as much as he could until his stomach ached from the effort and he had to stop and breathe again.

He would rest here. Just a little while, and then he would try to move again.

**

It was fully dark when he woke—night, not the cloud from Legerdemain, he thought.

His body still ached, but the pain had dulled to a steady throbbing rather than the sharp stabbing all over.

He took another drink of water and tried to push himself up.

So much pain. And he couldn't find his way in the dark, anyway.

His stomach growled. He needed to eat.

He'd lost his sword in his fall, but his pack was still strapped to his back. He felt around in it until he found his small knife and used it to cut some of the leaves from the plants that grew around him. He had no idea what he was eating or if it was poisonous, he just knew he needed something in his stomach.

After several minutes of munching on whatever was in reach, his stomach calmed some, and he managed to move away from the stream to the shelter of a tree. He wrapped his blanket around himself and slept.

A gray dawn greeted him when he awoke. There was still a little light this far away from the source of the darkness. Enough to see by. And his pain had eased enough that he was able to pull himself to his feet.

The stream wasn't too fast or deep to cross, so he carefully picked his way across, stopping on the other side to gather more leaves and mushrooms and other plants and stow them in his pack. He then refilled his waterskin. He didn't know what the foliage would be like further on, or when he would come to another stream.

He closed his eyes and tried to picture his vision in his mind. He still didn't know exactly where to go. He still had only his instinct to follow.

But suddenly it was clear. He felt it stronger than he had before, the calling of his vision.

Almost due north now.

And he was close. Just beyond the next ridge. There would be a forested valley, but not a large one, and just coming up the hill on the other side of that valley, he would find what he was looking for.

He took a deep breath and forced his feet to start moving. His body still burned with the pain of his injuries, but somehow they seemed easier to bear now that he knew he was so close.

The other side of the canyon was far less steep and not nearly as high as the one he'd rolled down. Within a few hours, he'd entered the forest, and soon after that, the ground began sloping away again, down into the next valley. Another stream flowed at the bottom of this one, and there were a few fish swimming in a small pool. He built a fire, caught some fish, and allowed himself the luxury of a short nap after eating.

Though the sky was dark, he guessed it to be about midafternoon when he started out again.

The pull of his destination grew stronger with every step, and energy coursed through him, refreshing him and easing the pain of his muscles and bruises.

Ahead, the trees seemed to thin, and he hurried his steps.

He broke out of the line of trees all at once into a huge clearing. Even the grasses and flowers seemed subdued here. The clearing was circled by huge stone pillars, and in the very center stood what seemed to be a massive stone table. This was the place—what had Ada called it? The cairn.

He stepped forward, past the line of stone pillars.

Warmth flooded through him. He hadn't even acknowledged the chill from the cold mountain air in his hurry to reach his destination, but now he realized how numb his body had become as the air that flowed around him, feeling like a room with a cozy fire, enveloped him.

Something else seemed to charge the air.

He recognized the sensation from his training sessions.

Magic.

Magic was concentrated here like he'd never imagined. If he, who had almost no magical ability whatsoever, could feel it, what must it be like for someone like his mother or Ada who were so powerful?

He closed his eyes and went through the steps to channel magic, forming a light in his hand.

Magic pulsed through him, energizing him and flooding him with heat. A light burst forth from his hand, illuminating the whole clearing.

He walked toward the stone table in the center of the clearing.

Something was written on it, etched in the stone—words he couldn't read.

At least… not at first. But as he stared at them, even though they were still written in an ancient script, their meaning filled his mind.

When the darkness reigns
Then the hate shall bind
The hearts of one and all
Until the light is found

Those who triumph fall
Those who seek shall find

Those who rule shall serve
The servant, ruler of all

The begotten of the dragons
Beloved of the Creator
Who bears the Dragon Stone
The Deliverer of the World

He recognized it. He'd memorized the prophecy from his earliest days. But this was only a small part of it. Why only write the last three stanzas on the stone?

The answer became clear even as he thought about it.

Because that was what was coming true in this moment. Darkness reigned. He could only imagine the hate that bound those living under the sorceress's control.

He didn't understand most of the rest, but deep inside, he knew he was the one who must find the light, so that the sorceress who ruled would fall.

The stone that made up the top of the table seemed to be separate from the stones that held it up. Using the magic that now flowed freely through him, he lifted the stone, moving it to the side to reveal a cavern.

He knew what he had to do. Without another thought, he jumped into the hole.

The Dungeons

Sharp, searing pain jolted through Ada's leg, up through her whole body, sending her crashing to the floor, body spasming.

Lysli stalked closer and kicked her.

The kick hardly registered amid the pain from the cuff, other than to reveal that Lysli couldn't contain her anger. Usually her punishments were methodical, calculated. But this—this was rage.

"Where is it?" Lysli demanded.

Ada opened her mouth to speak but could not find words, her mind was so clouded by pain.

The cuff eased slightly, enough for her to catch her breath and respond. "Where is what? I don't know what you're talking about."

"The amulet," Lysli growled. "You've been keeping it from me."

"What amulet?"

Lysli kicked again. "Quit playing with me! I know you have it. I've been reading the histories, and in every account, someone uses it to perform powerful magic. It is the key to taking this land—to healing it! Why don't you want that? Why are you hiding it from me?"

Ada wheezed. "If you've been reading the histories, then you know the amulet is passed down to the heir. I don't have it."

"The queen must have been wearing it when I killed her. Which means you would have gotten it when she died."

106

"Perhaps it was destroyed with her."

"No. It doesn't work like that. The spell I used absorbs magical energy."

"And the amulet was a magical artifact. You must have taken it when you took hers."

"Don't you think I know the difference? Don't you think I would've known if I'd gotten that much power? I would've felt it! I wouldn't be dealing with the nonsense I'm facing now if I had! You took it, I know you did!"

"If you did not absorb its power, perhaps the queen gave it to her son."

That gave Lysli pause. She seemed to be considering it. Enough that the pain from the cuff dulled to a steady thrum rather than a searing fire.

"If that's so," Lysli said at last, "why hasn't he used it against me?"

"I told you, he has almost no magical ability. He would need to be able to channel it to use the amulet at all. He's not powerful enough."

The pain in the cuff faded.

"Come," Lysli ordered.

Ada struggled to her feet and limped after the other woman, down the hallway to where Lysli had set up a magical chamber, much like the one Ada had downstairs.

"Prepare the water for Seeing," Lysli demanded.

Ada obeyed. Even the dried herbs were dying. The magic that coursed through all of nature felt weak. Strained. Like the world itself had given up.

Lysli followed Ada's instructions on how to See, and stared for a long time at the water. Ada couldn't tell by her expression what, if anything, she Saw.

After a long time, Lysli looked up. "Where are the dungeons?"

Ada's heart clutched.

She'd done it. Despite everything Ada had done to protect the Amulet, Lysli had found it. And Ada had no choice but to comply with her demands.

"This way," she said.

She walked slowly, hobbling on her ancient feet, stalling as much as possible, though the few minutes she gained were surely useless in the long run.

She led the way to the regular dungeons. Not the secret ones beyond the kitchen where the amulet actually was. It was only a matter of time until Lysli figured it out, but the longer she could stall…

She sighed. What was the point? Troy was still gone. More people died every day. The world was still dark, and it might be beyond the point where it could be saved.

Lysli spent the next several hours slowly walking up and down the cavernous tunnels of the empty dungeons.

Ada could feel the magic pulsing out from her, like a beacon, as she sought the amulet. She seemed to believe Ada didn't know where it was, because she didn't ask or try to force Ada to tell her anything. She clearly believed she could find it on her own, and Ada was happy to let her try.

At long last, Lysli sighed deeply. "It's not here. And yet it must be. I Saw it very clearly. It's hidden in a dungeon."

"Perhaps Troy escaped to Cadalania or Kir and has it hidden with him," Ada suggested.

Lysli shook her head. "It's here. I know it is. I just have to figure out where."

Ada followed her slowly up the winding staircase to the main level. The magic still pulsed out of her periodically.

Ada held her breath as they passed the kitchen, praying that they would pass by without…

Lysli stopped, her head jerking up. She stared down the hallway that led through the kitchen.

Ada's heart thundered. That way led to the secret dungeons. And almost as dire, it led to the storage room where Altya had her secret office.

She'd tried to remain ignorant, but Ada couldn't keep from knowing where Altya was and what she was doing. She was just glad that Lysli didn't suspect anything, or know that there was something worth asking about.

"This way," Lysli said.

Ada followed her down the hallway.

The servants in the kitchen stopped and stared as Lysli entered the room. Some of them had the presence of mind to curtsy, but most of them just stared in horrified wonder.

Katte caught Ada's eye, her gaze terrified, questioning whether or not Altya had been found out.

Ada gave her a quick shake of her head to let her know Altya's secret was safe—so far—and Katte nodded. She quickly composed herself and stepped forward. "To what do we owe the honor, your Majesty?" she asked.

Lysli barely looked at her, her eyes gazing down the hallway beyond. "Where does that lead?"

"Just storage rooms and cellars," Katte answered. "May I help you find something?"

Lysli ignored her and started down the hallway.

Katte's face blanched and Ada tossed her another reassuring glance.

Taking the hint, Katte turned back to the dough she was kneading on the counter. "Come on, then," she said to the others. "Dinner won't make itself."

The sounds of bustling in the kitchen started up again as Ada followed Lysli down the long hallway.

Lysli didn't even glance twice at the door that led to Altya's office. Her focus remained ahead.

Straight toward the door that led to the hidden dungeons.

They came to the door and Lysli tried it. It was locked, of course, but that didn't stop her. She shoved it with magic and broke it open, then strode down the narrow stairs to the landing, forming a glowing ball in her hand to light the way as she went.

Three passages led off from the landing room, going to three levels of dungeon that sat on top of one another.

Lysli paused and stared at all three in turn, magic pulsing through her as she studied each one.

Ada held out hope that she would choose the wrong one, but she didn't. She stalked toward the one leading to the lowest level and made her way down the stairs. Ada followed, though she knew what they would find.

At the bottom of the stairs was a long hallway, cells on either side. Lysli walked slowly down until she came to the third one from the end on the right.

Inside, wrapped in a bundle of old rags, lay the amulet.

Lysli picked it up and unwrapped it. Her eyes widened and her mouth stretched in a horrific smile. She held the amulet up, her light reflecting in it, making it glow with a pulsing violet radiance.

"At last," she said.

She turned to look at Ada. "Now, you will die."

The Portal

Cold stone walls lined the huge cavern. Troy took a moment to let his eyes adjust to the darkness that seemed to swallow up the magical light he'd created. The drop hadn't been too far, and he'd landed on his feet with not more than a little shock running through his him when he hit the bottom. And yet, the cavern seemed to go on forever.

How could it be so large, so expansive, and not have caused him injury when he jumped into it?

Glancing up, he saw the dim, gray light of the hole he'd jumped through far above. Too far. He hadn't fallen that far. And now… now, how would he ever get back up there?

That was a problem for another time, however. Now, he needed to do what he came to do.

Which was… what?

He had no idea.

He only knew he was supposed to be here, at this moment.

He drew more magic into himself and made the light brighter. He walked toward the wall in front of him, gazing up at the distant shadows that hid the ceiling. He made a slow circuit around, looking for something, anything that might reveal to him what he was supposed to do next.

He'd made almost a complete circuit around the cave when he stopped. The wall in front of him... shifted somehow.

What was it? What was happening to it?

He could still see the rock wall, but there seemed to be something in front it. Almost like looking through a stream to see the rocks on the bottom. Slowly, tentatively, he reached out his hand to touch the liquid wall.

It rippled under his touch, the substance thick, warm, and almost viscous under his fingers.

He reached further, trying to touch the rocks on the other side, but couldn't reach them.

Should he try to go through? Should he try to break it—maybe try to use magic on it?

He continued to touch the strange bubble with his fingertips, weighing his options, hoping to come up with a reasonable plan of action.

Movement caught his eye and he directed the light toward it. Beyond the bubble, in a dark corner, something moved almost imperceptibly. Like a shadow shifting in a candle's gentle flicker. He took a step closer to try to see it better.

The shadow wasn't just a dark corner—it was a tunnel, and something was emerging from it.

No, not something, someone.

A man. He was old, with a gray beard that reached nearly down to his middle and deep lines in his face. He moved slowly, so slowly that at first Troy wondered whether he was terribly frail, even though he seemed to be in good health despite his age. After a moment, however, Troy realized that it wasn't that the man's movements were slow, exactly. They were fluid and normal—except that whatever was on the other side of the bubble was slowed down somehow. As though time was stretched out.

After what seemed like an eternity, the man drew close to the bubble-like barrier and pressed his hand against it. It didn't go through, though—the barrier didn't ripple and the man's hand didn't penetrate the way Troy's did.

Troy placed his hand in the same spot and pushed through the barrier. He watched as his own hand seemed to almost stop, to move with that same agonizing slowness that he'd watched the old man move with, even though he continued to push through with the same force on this side of the barrier.

His hand emerged from the other side—he could feel the cool sting of the air in the cavern on the other side, a shock after the warm, gooey feel of the bubble.

The old man touched his fingers and smiled.

He mouthed the words, *It is time*, then slowly turned away.

Troy pulled his hand back.

What now? There was no way to get the old man's attention without going all the way through, and if the old man couldn't get through, he didn't want to risk not being able to come back.

And yet, the man had seemed happy. *It is time.* What did that mean? Was he supposed to go through? Was he supposed to wait? How long? At the rate the old man traveled, it could be hours or even days before he returned, even if he was only going to the next room.

At any rate, Troy couldn't just leave. He was led here for a reason, and the old man seemed to know what was going on. There was nothing else to do but wait.

He sat on the floor and opened his pack.

Immediately, the light went out. He'd dropped his concentration on the magic and lost it.

He could still see the other side of the barrier, though. A torch hung from the wall there, illuminating the cavern on that side.

But it didn't penetrate to where he was.

It was the strangest sensation—he couldn't see his own hand in front of his face from the darkness of the cavern he was in, yet he could clearly see the rock wall that formed the cavern on the other side and the flicker of the flames of the torch and the footprints in the dust on the floor.

The footprints.

That was odd.

Troy got up again to look. He could see the very human prints the old man had left when he walked out, but there were others, too. Not human. Huge, three-toed prints had left craters in the dust. Some kind of massive beast had walked in and out of this cavern.

Did the old man know? Was he in danger? Should Troy go try to find him?

But no. The man clearly came here often. The beast, whatever it was, had not disturbed the torch on the wall, and the man had not seemed at all fearful.

Troy sat down again. He remade the ball of light and tried to think about the things his mother and Ada had taught him about magic. There was a way to fix the spell so that it stood on its own…

There.

He attached the globe of light to the wall of the cavern so it shone down on him without him having to maintain it and opened his pack. The bits of food he'd collected by the river made a good enough dinner. He wished he had more, but at least it was enough to sate the gnawing hunger in his stomach.

The old man had not returned, and Troy's journey wore on him. His muscles were still sore, and the exertion of the day had taken its toll on him. He pulled out his blanket and lay down, hoping to get a little rest before the old man returned.

He didn't know how long he slept, but he felt refreshed when he woke.

He looked across the barrier into the other cavern. Still nothing.

How much longer should he wait? Glancing up, he found the hole where he'd jumped through. The sky was light—sort of. Dawn? Or was it midday, but the sorceress's darkness had spread this far?

He couldn't tell from here.

Something moved, and he turned his attention back to the cavern on the other side of the barrier.

The old man came into view, walking at that same agonizingly slow pace. Behind him came something else. At first, Troy couldn't tell what it was, and it moved as slowly as the old man, but little by little it came far enough into the light that he could begin to distinguish it.

It was a beast, more terrifying than any in the forest that surrounded Legerdemain.

It stood three times the old man's height. It had a sort of leathery, scaly skin, but rather than the greens and browns of the lizards or snakes he knew, it was a bright, almost iridescent red. Its head had a series of horn-like protrusions that jutted out from its skull, almost like a crown, and fangs showed when it opened its mouth. He'd seen something like it before—on one of the tapestries in the Council room. The thing was monstrous, but it did not seem vicious. It followed the old man into the cavern, then looked across the barrier directly at Troy, its eyes showing its intelligence.

It is time.

Troy felt the words reverberating inside him.

He looked at the beast, and it nodded at him.

What did it mean? What was he supposed to do?

The old man reached out a hand and touched the barrier.

Troy reached for him, through the bubble, and the old man grabbed his hand, but this time he didn't let go. This time, he stepped closer. Troy stepped back, pulling the old man with him. And the old man passed through the barrier.

A rich, vibrant laugh erupted from the man's throat when he emerged on Troy's side of the barrier. He pulled Troy into a deep embrace. "Thank you, Son," he said. "We have been waiting a long time for you."

"I... I don't even know what I'm doing here," Troy said. "I was led here, by magic, I think. Who are you? And what is that?"

The man smiled. "My name is Cornan. And that is a dragon."

The Dragons

"Help me," Cornan said. "We must get the others out."

"The others?" Troy asked.

Cornan nodded toward the barrier. Behind the red dragon who had followed Cornan, the cavern began to fill with others of its kind, in all colors. Brilliant blues, purples, yellows, greens—every shade imaginable—they all crammed into the space behind the barrier.

Cornan reached his hand through the barrier and gripped the large talon that the red dragon held out to him. With Cornan's touch, the dragon was able to penetrate the barrier and walk through.

It bowed before Troy when it emerged. "Thank you. My name is Covelli." Though he didn't quite know how he knew, Troy could immediately tell she was female.

"I am Troy," he said. "I am the prince of a land called Legerdemain."

"The prince?" Covelli said. "Then you are the descendant of Cerik?"

Troy nodded.

"Grandson? Great-grandson?"

"It must be longer than that," Cornan said. "It was more than a hundred years from the founding when I left, and I was a young man then."

Covelli nodded. "Of course, you are right. I forget how time has played tricks on us all. If he is here, it has been a full Age." She turned back to Troy. "How long has it been since the founding of Legerdemain?"

Troy thought back to his history lessons. "Nearly a thousand years," he said.

Covelli nodded slowly. "Yes, I suppose that makes sense," she said. "I can hardly believe it has been that long. Let us get the others out, and then you can tell me what has happened in the world during the last Age."

Troy nodded and joined Covelli and Cornan in reaching through the barrier to grasp the hands—or, rather, the claws—of the other dragons.

One by one, they came through. "Fly to the surface and wait for us at the cairn," Covelli told them.

It was only after the first one took flight that Troy realized they all had wings, tucked in against their backs until they launched into the air. He gaped in astonishment as the first few ascended before turning back to help the rest of them through.

"So… you were trapped here?" he asked eventually.

"Not exactly," Covelli said. "We came here intentionally. We called it the Long Sleep, although now we realize it wasn't really a sleep. We knew we were not destined to be in the world during this Age, so we came here to wait."

Troy pulled a green dragon through the barrier and waited until it flew out of the cave before asking, "Where is 'here', exactly?"

"It's sort of like a garden, I suppose. On the other side of the portal, the cavern opens up into another land, but it is small, at least compared to the earth." She pulled another dragon through and it flew up to meet the others. "There was plenty of room for us, but everything was sort of in stasis. No one gave birth or really did much beyond living day to day in a garden that never needed tending. We knew, according to the prophecies, that we would return at the end of an Age, but our role is unclear."

"I believe it is to help us fight a great war," Troy said. "There is a sorceress, one who has come into our land. A great darkness has spread, blotting out the sun and causing everything to die. I don't know what she plans to do—I left before she could find me—but the darkness has been spreading, so I know she must still live. She wields great magic, and even our most powerful sorceresses apparently could not stop her."

117

"Yes, that fits with the prophecy," Covelli said. "Tell me about this sorceress."

"I don't know much," Troy said. "She came into our land with no warning. Almost as though she appeared out of nowhere. She besieged the city and demanded we give her control. My mother, the queen, refused. She called a Council meeting, and it was decided to fight her, but I was not allowed to join. My mother wanted to keep me hidden in the castle, but Ada showed me a secret way out and sent me here."

At that, Cornan's head snapped up, and he stared at Troy. "Ada lives?"

Troy looked at him. How could he possibly... "Yes," he said slowly. "She is my mother's advisor."

"As she was the advisor to every king and queen who lived before my time," Cornan said. A soft, wistful smile spread over his face beneath is flowing beard. "Tell me, is she still young and beautiful?"

Troy's eyes widened. He had trouble picturing Ada as either of those things. "No. She's old. My mother said she was just as old when she first met her, almost eighteen years ago. I have no idea how old she actually is."

"If you are correct in your calculations of how long it has been since your country's founding," Covelli said, "she is nearly one thousand years old."

Troy almost dropped the claw of the dragon he was pulling through the portal. "That's not... how is that possible?"

A deep laugh rumbled in Covelli's chest. "I always knew Yridessa was a powerful dragon, but this exceeds even my expectations. It will be good to see her again."

Ada—Yridessa—a dragon—what?

"All will be explained in time," Covelli said. "Once everyone is through the portal, we will discuss what we must do next."

The process seemed to take hours. So many dragons filed through the entrance to the cave, a line that never seemed to end. There wasn't enough room in the other cavern, nor along the breadth of the barrier itself, to invite others to join in pulling them through, so Troy, Cornan, and Covelli were the only ones to continue the job of transporting them.

At last, the last few dragons filed into the cavern and the three pulled them through.

The last dragon through the barrier was a small, yellow dragon.

"There is no one left in the garden, Amylla?" Covelli asked.

"I am the last," Amylla said, bowing.

"Thank you. Will you kindly carry Prince Troy to the cairn?"

"Of course," Amylla said. She knelt and put her shoulders close to the ground.

Covelli did the same, and Cornan climbed on her back. Troy followed the old man's example and climbed on Amylla's back. It was like riding a very large horse, though somehow both more terrifying and more reassuring. Amylla's back was broad and sturdy, and the muscles moved smoothly. Besides which, she could talk, so he could communicate with her. But there were no reins to hold onto, no saddle to keep him in place, and she launched straight up toward the hole in the cavern.

Troy clung to her, gripping her rough scales under his fingers and squeezing his legs together.

She laughed. "Don't worry, I won't let you fall," she said.

She darted through the opening—it was larger than when Troy had opened it. The other dragons must have widened the hole when they got out.

The rest of the dragons stood around the center stone, staying within the bounds of the clearing, marked by the tall, stone pillars. Most of them looked nervously at the sky, now fully covered by the sorceress's magic.

Covelli looked at him. "Please tell us what this is, and what it means."

Troy again explained, this time to the whole group, about the sorceress who had come to take their land.

"Thank you," Covelli said when he finished. She turned to face the dragons. "We knew this day would come when we entered the Long Sleep. There are no guarantees to the outcome of this battle—it is a thing that cannot be Seen. We were at peace in the Garden, and any who wish to go back there will be safe from the coming war. If you choose to go, go in peace. For those who wish to fight this sorceress, sleep, for in the morning we go home."

The Cuff

A shock of pain, like having her body dipped in a blazing fire, ripped through Ada, but she didn't die.

Lysli snarled and tried again, pulling magic through the amulet and directing it at Ada.

"Why won't this work?" she asked.

She wasn't really looking for an answer, of course. But Ada told her anyway. "It is attached to the blood heir of this nation. You may be able to use it, but it will not work for you the same way it will work for him. And you will not be able to use it against him. If you try, it will destroy you."

"Attached to the blood heir. So that means it is bound by a blood vow, yes? I learned much about blood magic in the Barbarian lands. Blood vows can be broken. Come."

She stalked to her chamber where her magical workshop was. She pulled a handful of herbs from her stores and set them on the table. She then placed a series of gemstones along the table, starting with a bright yellow citrine and moving in color to peridot, emerald, sapphire, amethyst, ruby, and garnet.

She pulled magic from the air and channeled it into the citrine, filling it up until it held all it could contain, then did the same for the others.

When she finished, she placed a bright, clear diamond on the table next to the citrine and the amulet next to that, so the amulet started the line.

She then mixed her herbs into a potion. Ada didn't recognize the potion itself, but the mint could be used to weaken spells, the thyme could be used to dull pain, and the rosemary could be used to counteract some spells. Together, they would make a potent concoction to aid in her attempt to break the spell.

When she finished, Lysli grabbed Ada's hand. She pulled a small dagger from her belt and sliced Ada's palm. Ada recoiled and tried to pull her hand away, but the pain in her cuff stopped her from moving at all.

Lysli squeezed Ada's hand, dripping several drops of blood onto the amulet.

"It won't work," Ada said. "That's not how this spell was made."

"Perhaps not," Lysli said, unconcerned.

Ada's bravado faltered. In reality, she had no idea how the spell was done. Yliva had prepared the potion and the amulet was formed by her and the first king, using magic along with Cerik's vow. It was a powerful magic, but Lysli was a powerful sorceress. If anyone could break it, she could. And this... this might work.

Lysli began to chant in the ancient language while she pulled magic through the potion and gathered it up from the gems she'd put it into.

Her skin seemed to glow with a dark radiance as she channeled all the magic into the diamond. Finally, she picked up the diamond and aimed the many threads of magic into the amulet.

An explosion like lightning striking dry timber shot out from the amulet, sending a shockwave that sent Ada and Lysli both flying backward from the table.

Ada landed on her backside and slid until she crashed into the wall.

It took several moments before her head cleared enough for her to open her eyes.

Lysli lay against another wall, her eyes still closed.

The amulet sat on the table, pulsing with a pale violet light. What did that mean? Did it work?

Ada slowly pulled herself to her feet. She hobbled to the table and touched the amulet. Magic thrummed inside it, but she couldn't tell whether it was because it had accepted the spell or rejected it.

Lysli still lay unmoving. She couldn't be dead, could she? That would be too much to hope for.

A soft moan escaped her lips. Not dead, then. She would awake at any moment, and if her spell had worked, then she would kill Ada.

Ada quickly ran through her options. She could try to run, but she was too old, too slow. Besides, she still wore the cuff, which meant Lysli could track her or simply force her to return.

The cuff.

She had to get the cuff off. And she might just have a way.

But she had to work quickly, before Lysli woke.

She grabbed the bowl with the potion from the table and doused the cuff with it, then threw it across the room in the other direction so it would look like it was flung aside from Lysli's spell.

Then the diamond. She picked it up. Magic remained inside, stored instead of channeled. Even if Ada couldn't channel magic herself with the cuff on, perhaps she could direct what magic remained in the diamond into her cuff.

She held the diamond against the seam where the cuff linked together around her ankle and pushed.

The cuff burned, as though fighting against her attempts to wield magic, but she fought through the pain and continued to try to force the magic out of the diamond.

All at once, the cuff shattered, breaking off her ankle and falling in pieces on the floor.

Ada gasped and pulled magic into herself, filling up with power for the first time since Lysli had placed the cuff on her.

The power felt like a breath of fresh, clean air from high up in the sky as she soared above the earth back when she was a dragon.

Lysli started to move, and Ada thrust a wave of magic at her to bind her.

Not quickly enough.

Lysli deflected the spell and returned with one of her own.

Ada couldn't stay to duel with her. She grabbed the amulet from the table and turned to run, but couldn't. The amulet burned her hand, pulling toward Lysli.

Lysli laughed, a harsh, cruel sound.

Was she drawing the amulet toward herself or was the amulet itself drawn to her?

Either way, Ada couldn't fight it.

She released the amulet and ran, darting down the hallway as fast as her old legs could carry her, before Lysli had a chance to capture or kill her. She ducked into a servants' corridor and made her way quickly downstairs. Perhaps she could hide in the storage areas or dungeons.

No, Lysli would no doubt scour the castle for her. She had to get out.

She couldn't risk going anywhere Lysli's guards might be. So she made her way to the lowest level, to the Council room.

She locked and barred the door and snuck behind the tapestry into the hidden tunnel that she'd sent Troy through.

It was nearing dusk, as close as she could tell beyond the black cloud, by the time she emerged outside the castle walls.

She breathed deeply, but the air outside was just as musty and smelling of death as the stale air inside the tunnel.

And now she didn't know what to do or where to go. Lysli was convinced that killing Ada would give her the power she desired, and there was no way to convince her otherwise. At least not without telling her the truth—that Troy was the key.

Where was Troy now?

He wasn't dead—of that she was quite certain. He was the last of his line. She would've felt it if he'd died. Even now that Lysli controlled the amulet, he was still bonded to the land. It was still his blood that would give Lysli the power over this land, although even that would not heal or restore anything. Lysli's power would only grow darker. Her extended lifetime would not give her the power she sought. She would be empress of death, nothing more.

But of course, she would not hear that. She would continue to kill everyone and everything until there was nothing left and it was too late to fix it. Unless she could be stopped. And now Troy was the only one who could stop her.

She had to find Troy.

He'd gone to the cairn. She started to walk north, toward the mountains.

She'd almost arrived at the desolate North Village when something washed over her—the sensation of magic, pulsing down from high above. Pure, raw, unfiltered. Untouched by the darkness.

Could Lysli feel it, too? And if she could, did she have any idea what it meant?

Ada laughed, the sound rising into the sky and echoing against the blackness.

The Confrontation

Altya paused in her instructions to her guards, suddenly short of breath.

What was that? What had happened?

The men and women before her were the ones tasked with freeing the magic users the empress had enslaved. What started with a few had become more than a dozen who were free and awaiting her orders. They'd assembled to make a plan of attack, congregating in Altya's small storage room office.

But now, they all stood before her, silent, mouths gaping, blood draining from their faces.

"What was that?" Maryn asked, her voice hoarse.

Apparently they'd all felt it, too, that sensation like a gust of wind blowing through them, except all was still.

"It was magic," one of the others said.

"Where did it come from?" Altya asked. "Does the empress know where we are? What we're doing? Was it an attack?"

Maryn shook her head. "Not an attack. It was… new. Or very, very old."

"What does that mean? Are we in danger?"

"I don't know," Maryn said. "I don't think so. At least not from that. But if the empress felt it, she will feel threatened, and that does put us all at risk."

A scream reverberated through the castle, shaking the very walls.

"She felt it," Maryn whispered. "She will be coming for us. Draining the life of everyone in sight to fuel her own dark magic."

"What do we do?" Altya asked.

"Get as many civilians out of the castle as possible," Maryn said. "Send them to the villages and tell them to hide. We are going to be at war. If we lose, it will truly be the end."

"And what are the chances that we can win?" Altya asked.

Maryn smiled. "For the first time since the empress invaded our land, I have hope."

That was enough for Altya. She sent for Katte.

"Take all the servants, all the children, anyone who does not wish to or is not able to fight, and get to the South Village."

"I wish to stay and help, my lady," Katte protested.

"You are my most trusted general," Altya said. "I need you to ensure the safety of our people, as many as possible. Get them out and hide. If we win... well, if we win, you'll know."

Katte breathed deeply and bowed. "As you say, my lady."

Within the hour, Katte had all the servants and others who had taken refuge in the castle gathered by the back servants' entrance.

Maryn had managed to find a few more of the enslaved magic users and was working to remove their cuffs. Those who could use magic and all the soldiers still living huddled nearby, awaiting orders. Altya would've given anything to add Ada to their numbers, but the empress never let Ada out of her sight, and there had been no opportunity. But they would make do with what they had.

"What will we do if the empress sees us trying to leave?" Katte asked.

"She will be otherwise occupied," Altya said. She nodded to Maryn and the others. "It's time."

Katte led the servants and civilians out the back entrance and Altya led the warriors and magicians up the long flights of stairs toward the throne room.

An aura of darkness permeated the hallways, more so than before. Like a thick cloud of fog that made it nearly impossible to see, even with torches burning on all the walls.

The air felt thicker, heavier, more sinister with every step. In another moment they would be in the presence of the empress. And she would likely try to kill them all.

Altya just hoped Maryn and the others were right, that what they'd felt earlier was a sign that something had shifted. That they now stood a chance.

They approached the door to the throne room where two soldiers stood guard. Altya held her head high. "I am Lady Altya, Regent of Legerdemain in the absence of his Majesty, King Troy. I request an audience with the empress."

The two guards stared at her, silent, unmoving for a long moment.

"Who put you in charge?" one of them asked at last.

"The King's chief advisor, Lady Ada," Altya answered.

The relief washing over the guard was palpable as his shoulders relaxed and his lips turned up in a smile. "Can I... can I join you?"

Altya nodded her head. "Welcome." She turned to the other. "And you?"

He gulped. "The empress will kill us all."

"It's very likely," Altya agreed. "But she is going to do that anyway. This way, it will be quick, and we may be able to kill her in the process."

"Do you really think it's possible?"

"We're about to find out," Altya said. "Open the door."

The guards pulled open the two doors, then fell into place behind her with the other soldiers.

The empress whirled around, her face looking haggard... old. Bodies littered the floor around her. Her eyes narrowed. "Who are you?"

Altya lifted her chin, forcing her voice to sound braver than she felt. "I am Lady Altya, Regent of Legerdemain. We have come to take our kingdom back from your rule."

She held forth one of the cuffs that Maryn had removed from one of the magic users. "Surrender, and you will live."

The empress laughed, her voice bitter and cruel. "You cannot kill me."

She stretched her hand toward Altya and squeezed her fist.

Altya's chest constricted, as though a she were being pressed under a heavy weight. Maryn jumped in front of her, a glow of magic pulsing from her hands, as she deflected the spell the empress had used.

All the magic users joined hands, lining up on either side of Maryn. Her magic grew brighter, and for a moment, the empress looked panicked, like she feared their power.

But then the spell snapped, and Maryn staggered backward, her face paling and her body going rigid before collapsing to the floor, her body a lifeless husk.

The empress smiled and turned to the next one in line.

The next magic user was a man in his middle years whose name Altya did not know. Instead of trying to deflect the spell, however, he opened his arms and embraced it, then channeled the magic upward.

It only lasted a few seconds before he, too, was killed, but it was enough to make a crack in the ceiling that began to spread.

That distracted the empress from her spell long enough for the magic users to regroup. But they only had moments to launch a spell at the empress before the crack widened, opening to the sky above, and growing wider by the moment until it stretched down the walls, separating the entire castle into halves.

The empress screamed as though in pain, her eyes focused on something above, something only she could see.

With a cloud of smoke, she disappeared. To where, Altya couldn't say, but she was away from the castle, which threatened to collapse on them at any moment.

"Everyone out," Altya ordered. "Reconvene at the tavern by the west wall. The empress still reigns, but we have some time before she will strike again."

The floor shook and the stones on the walls crumbled. "Go, quickly!"

Altya was the last one to leave, making sure all her followers made it out first, and checking servants' quarters for any who lingered before making her way to the courtyard.

She watched in awe and horror as the castle imploded, collapsing in on itself until it was a huge heap of stone. She waited until the dust settled, and then made her way to the tavern. They'd won a small victory, but the war was far from over.

The War – Part One

Dawn poked its thin tendrils between the mountains and the darkness.

Troy woke to the sounds of the monstrous dragons stirring and talking in low tones.

"There is not much to eat," one of them said to Covelli, the dragon who appeared to be the leader. "The animals are mostly dead. There are carcasses everywhere, but most of them are rotted far beyond what is safe to eat."

"That's unfortunate," Covelli said. "However, we will be fine until we can rectify whatever is going on." She looked toward Troy. "Ah, you are awake. Good. Please, join us."

Troy joined the circle of dragons as they convened around Covelli.

"We will depart immediately for the city. I imagine the sorceress has felt our presence by now, but she will not know what to expect. We will fly in a straight line until we get to the base of the mountains, then we will send a scout to the human habitations to see what can be learned."

She turned to Troy. "You will know better how to interpret what is happening among the humans than we will, so you will go with whoever we send as a scout. Do not worry, however. You will be protected."

Troy nodded. He probably should've been afraid, but he wasn't. These creatures were more powerful than anything he had ever seen or even heard of. And he could use magic now.

At least... he could when he was in this clearing. Would his ability fade once he left this circle? A wave of panic shot through him at the thought. If he didn't have magic, would he be defenseless?

But no, that was not a reasonable fear. He would be with the dragons, and they were inherently magical. Besides, once he got back home, he could use a sword. It might not be much defense against the sorceress's magic, but he could use it against her soldiers, and the dragons could deal with the sorceress.

"Climb on my back," Covelli instructed. Troy pulled himself up and straddled her neck ridges, then held on as she launched into the sky.

The feeling of flying was even more majestic as they soared over the mountain than it had been leaping out of the cave. Covelli's wings beat in a steady rhythm, her body undulating under him as she soared. Below, Troy watched the landscape he'd spent so many days traversing pass by in minutes. The canyon where Sir Kire had died and he had almost done the same. The many, many peaks and valleys through which he'd wandered up and down.

And at last, the final peak, at the bottom of which lay the forest that stretched around the border of Legerdemain.

"We will take cover in the forest," Covelli said, starting her descent.

"I would not recommend hiding in the forest itself," Troy said into her ear. "There are monsters there—magical beasts created by my great uncle, who seized the throne from my grandfather."

"Very well," Covelli said. "There is no sense in taking unnecessary risks."

She flew down and landed just on the mountain side of the forest. The others followed her lead, spreading out along the side of the mountain.

"Your Highness, you will go with Amylla to discover what you can," Covelli said. She turned to the small, yellow dragon by her side. "Try not to make yourself known for as long as possible. Report back here if you can. But a blast of fire into the air will summon us to your side."

Amylla bowed her head in acknowledgment, and Troy slid from Covelli's back and climbed onto Amylla's.

Amylla launched into the air, skimming low over the trees, and then lower as she raced toward the city in the center of the country, skirting around the edge of the deserted North Village.

A lone figure emerged from one of the huts.

"Stop!" Troy shouted to Amylla.

The dragon banked and landed just south of the village. "What is it?" she asked.

"I'm not sure."

Amylla walked cautiously toward the person, who came toward them, walking on unsteady legs.

Troy slid from Amylla's back and ran toward her. "Ada!" he shouted.

Ada shuffled faster, and as she drew closer, he could see the tears running freely down her face. She pulled him into an embrace, her breath coming in deep, heavy sobs. "You're alive," she whispered over and over.

"I'm alive," Troy affirmed. "And I've brought help."

"I see that," Ada said, pulling away and turning to look at the dragon. She stepped forward and reached out her hand. "Amylla," she whispered. "It has been so long."

Amylla reared back, staring at Ada for a long moment before recognition dawned in her dark blue eyes. "Yridessa?"

Troy looked from one to the other as Ada laughed.

"I forgot you had already gone by the time I was turned," she said. "You have awoken from the Long Sleep."

Amylla nodded. "We never really slept. We were in a sort of other world, where, as we came to understand it, time moved very differently. In our world, it has been fifty or sixty years since we left."

"It has been nearly a thousand here," Ada said.

"What is happening in the city?" Troy interrupted. As much as he appreciated a thousand years of nostalgia, he had to know what was happening to his kingdom. "How is my mother?"

Ada turned to him, her eyes filling with tears once again. "Things are not good. Your mother is gone. The empress—as she calls herself— killed her and stole her magic, her essence, to give herself life."

"She has the spells of the gods?" Amylla gasped.

Ada nodded. "She has enslaved all the magic users, and is killing them one by one as she needs more power. She is trying to find Troy.

She believes he is the key to unlocking eternal life. And she has control of the amulet."

Troy choked.

His mother dead. The amulet that had been the catalyst for protecting their nation through countless generations, taken by the enemy.

But he had dragons.

"We must overwhelm her. Kill her," he said.

"That will not be so easily done," Ada said.

"The dragons are waiting on the other side of the forest. They are awaiting news from us, and then they will come to our aid."

"There is no time to waste," Ada said. "I have Seen the city—the empress is destroying everything. The castle is gone, the people are dying. Many of the sorcerers escaped from her cuffs, but they could only do so much against her."

"I will call the others," Amylla said. She leaned her head back and sucked in a deep breath, aiming her face toward the sky to send the signal that would alert Covelli and the others.

Before she could finish, her eyes bulged and she made a choking sound. A moment later, her body withered and shrank, and she became a dried husk that shattered when she collapsed to the ground, turning into tiny, sparkling bits of topaz.

Behind where she had been a moment before stood the empress. She transformed before Troy's eyes, her face growing more youthful and vibrant.

She laughed, a dark, mirthless cackle that rose up into the air. From around her neck hung the amulet—the amethyst encased in gold that had been passed down through the royal line for a thousand years. The magical icon that should've been Troy's.

It throbbed with violet light as the empress channeled magic through it.

She looked at him. "You must be the prince. They told me you couldn't use magic, but here you are—alive, and vibrating with power. And you brought me that beast, which contained more magic than anything I have ever felt. I am more powerful now than I have ever been, and when I break the hold you have over this land, I will rule all."

Ada launched some sort of spell at the empress, which the empress deflected easily.

133

Troy choked as her gaze fell on him once more. She stretched out her hand and the air seemed to tighten around him, squeezing, pulling. His very essence drained from him and poured into her.

He gasped for breath, but none came. His vision grew dark.

But he would not die in vain.

With the last dregs of his strength, he formed the one spell he knew well—the ball of light—and shot it into the air overhead.

And then everything went dark.

The War – Part Two

A flash of light pulsed out from Troy, creating a concussion that pushed Ada backward into the wall of the hut where she'd hidden.

A light like a ball of flame hovered in the air, burning through the thick darkness.

Troy lay on the ground, unmoving, and Lysli…

Where was Lysli?

Ada pushed herself up to a stand, her whole body aching with the effort.

She still didn't see Lysli, so she stumbled toward Troy and knelt beside him. She felt his face and neck and chest. He was alive, breathing shallowly, unconscious.

She patted his face. "Troy. Your Highness. Wake up!"

He groaned, but didn't wake.

From further down the field, something moved.

Ada looked up to see Lysli slowly pulling herself to a stand.

"Troy!" Ada shoved his shoulder, trying to rouse him.

Lysli took a slow step forward, then another. From around her neck, the amulet glowed. As she drew closer, she began to laugh.

"Troy!" Ada hissed.

"That was a good trick," Lysli said. "But it doesn't matter. I will still have him."

She reached out with magic. Ada blocked the spell, but could only hold Lysli off for a moment. Power coursed through her—the magic she'd stolen from Amylla had strengthened her, far more than stealing from any human had, and the amulet burned with stolen power.

In seconds, she'd shoved Ada's blocking spell out of the way and redirected her spell toward Troy.

His body trembled and started to turn a ghastly shade of ashen gray.

Ada lifted her arms to try to counter the spell again, but they wouldn't move. Magic refused to flow through her. It was as though all the magic in the land was now being diverted to Lysli.

In a final attempt to save him, Ada threw her body on top of Troy's.

This time, the spell seemed to work. Always before, it had drained Ada of some energy, but hadn't come close to killing her, as it had done to Queen Rina or any of the dozens of others Lysli had killed.

But now, she could feel the life draining out of her. A thousand years of memories and strength slowly ebbed away,

She gasped for breath, hoping only that her death might keep Lysli at bay long enough for help to arrive. Her head bobbed, and the world faded.

A flash of light from above woke her from the stupor she'd fallen into. Overhead was a sight she hadn't seen in nearly a thousand years.

A whole weyr of dragons flew toward them, flames erupting from their mouths.

The spell stopped as Lysli turned her attention to the beasts flying toward her. A sound escaped her lips, but it wasn't one of fear. It was laughter, demented and maniacal.

Lysli stretched out her hand and a moment later a dragon fell from the sky, crashing to the ground and exploding into fragments of sapphire and dust.

Lysli reached out again, and another dragon fell. With each dragon life she took, she grew stronger, making her spell that much more powerful, her ability to kill more efficient.

Ada rolled off Troy and pulled at whatever traces of magic she could grasp, funneling Healing into him. "Wake up, Troy!"

He blinked.

"That's it, come on," Ada said.

Overhead, the dragons rushed toward Lysli, only to be repelled by whatever shield spell she was using, and one by one, succumbing to her power-stealing death spell.

The darkness grew thicker the more she killed. No light filtered in from beyond the black clouds at all now. The only reason Ada could see anything at all was because Troy's ball of light spell still hung in the sky above them.

"Help me," Troy muttered.

Ada held out a hand to help him up.

He stood and breathed deeply. "I... I don't know what to do. I don't know how to stop her."

Lysli stumbled forward, as though she'd been shoved from behind. She whirled around, and Ada peered beyond her to see what she was looking at.

Coming up the road from the other direction was a cluster of sorcerers, led by one with a limp. Maryn. And the others she'd helped escape from the cuffs. They barraged Lysli from one side while the dragons kept coming at her from above.

But still she prevailed, her laugh echoing through the expanse of the country. "You fools! Do you not see? I am the most powerful sorceress in the world! I have the power of the gods! I *am* a god! You will all serve me, or you will die!"

A second group arrived within view—the empress's army of sorcerers. Those who were still enslaved as well as those who had come with her, the ones wearing the red cloaks. The red-cloaked sorcerers attacked Maryn's sorcerers, and those who were enslaved writhed on the ground in pain.

Beside Ada, Troy gasped for breath. "She just keeps getting stronger, and I don't know how to use magic."

"Yes, you do," Ada said, willing her voice to remain calm. "Try again."

Troy closed his eyes, his muscles straining from the effort.

"I can't do it. I felt it, up on the mountain, but here... here I can do nothing."

"You created that ball of light in the sky to summon the dragons. How did you do it?"

"I don't know, I... I just knew I had to."

"You have to now, your Highness. Look around. We can't hold her off. You must."

Troy tried again, and again gave up after a few moments.

"Again!" Ada yelled.

Another dragon, a dark red one—Ada thought it might be her cousin Capryl—fell from the sky and shattered into a thousand bits of garnet all around them.

Ada picked up one of the larger pieces. Magic swirled in the air, gathered from deep below the earth, where roots and stones had lain dormant for eons. Magic that Lysli hadn't known existed and hadn't touched. She channeled the magic into the garnet and handed it to Troy, then did the same with two more large pieces.

"Use that if you can't draw it yourself."

Troy pulled the magic into himself.

Ada pulled on the energy as well, lifting it up from the ground and directing it to Troy.

Troy dropped his arms and exhaled, his shoulders slumping in defeat. "I can't. I… I just can't."

Ada faced him. "You are the son of a powerful sorceress and a sorcerer whose bloodline was engineered to be the most powerful in the world. Lysli—she is nothing. She steals her power. That is the only way she has anything. Your power is your own. Now, use it!"

Lysli stepped closer, her body blazing with power, her face a skeletal horror as the magic drained from her continued use almost as fast as she stole it. She didn't seem to notice or care, however. Her teeth were bared in a terrifying grin as she continued to pull the power from her victims and walk slowly toward Troy.

"The old woman was right all along," she taunted. "You really are nothing. I thought the son of Jarok would at least give me a challenge, but you… you are weak. And now you are done."

The amulet around her neck blazed again, the light so bright it was almost white instead of purple. She lifted her hands to strike.

The Final Battle

Troy stumbled back.

The sorceress stalked toward him, laughing that maniacal laugh. The amulet—*his* amulet, since she had killed his mother—blazed with light.

Ada said she took it, made it hers.

But it wasn't hers. No matter how powerful her magic was, she couldn't have that. She couldn't break a thousand years of connection… could she?

Even if she could, then that meant the bond could be broken, which meant he could take it back. If only he knew how.

But he wasn't trained in magic. The lessons had never gone very far because he was always so unsuccessful. He was trained in swordplay. If he could challenge her to a duel, then maybe…

A duel.

That's what this was. It was duel using magic instead of swords, but it was still a duel. And he could fight a duel.

Sir Kire's words flooded over him. *The sword is a part of you. An extension of you. Your movements should flow freely, as naturally as waving your hand.*

Magic swirled around him and he pulled it toward himself, into himself. The garnets Ada had handed him pulsed almost as brightly as the amulet around the sorceress's neck.

140

The magic was an extension of himself. This was a duel.

Almost without conscious thought, a sword formed in his hands, forged of magic, blazing dark red, pulsing with power.

The sorceress narrowed her eyes, but didn't stop. She flung a spell at him.

Troy lifted the sword and blocked the spell, as he would block a blow from an opponent. Just a turn of his wrist to angle the blade and protect himself.

First rule of fencing—don't die.

He stepped back, using his magic blade to deflect spell after spell. If only he could use them against her...

Wait. Why couldn't he? With a real sword, he used his opponent's mistakes to find an opening. With magic, he could do the same thing.

Casting spells was wearing her out—he could see it in the way her movements became slower and her eyes narrowed in concentration.

Find a weakness and exploit it.

The sorceress aimed another spell at him, and this time, instead of just deflecting, he used the magic coursing through the sword to bounce the spell back at her.

It worked. The spell hit her, singeing her flesh. She yelped and jumped back, eyeing him. She cast another spell at him, and he again deflected it back to her, but this time she was ready. She caught it in the amulet, absorbing its power and drawing from it. This time, when she cast, she used the full force of the magic pulsing from the amulet to overwhelm him.

He morphed the sword into a shield that covered him, but the spell still burned him, scorching his skin like the time he'd tripped and his arm had fallen into the coals in the hearth when he was young.

Neither of them could keep this up much longer. Whoever ran out of energy first would succumb. The sorceress would not give up until one of them was dead, and she had the advantage. She held the amulet, the most powerful magical artifact perhaps in the world.

The amulet. That was the key, after all.

He tried to remember all the things he'd learned in his history lessons about how it was forged, what it had done, how the kings and queens before him had used it to save this land from threats.

One thing he remembered from his mother was that the amulet was linked by blood. The sorceress had broken that bond... or had she?

Perhaps she had just bent it. Perhaps he was still linked to it, despite whatever spell she had used to steal it.

Troy pulled himself to his full height and walked slowly toward the sorceress, remaking the magical sword blade in his hands.

"You have something that belongs to me," he said, nodding toward the amulet.

"It's mine now. It won't work for you now."

"You know nothing. You don't know where it came from or what it is or why it's important. You manipulated it, but it's not yours. The power that connects me to it goes beyond your understanding."

He stepped closer, using the magical sword to put her on the defensive.

She stepped back and channeled magic into the amulet, but before she could strike, Troy lunged, stabbing the sword into the amulet.

The sorceress staggered backwards, clutching at the amulet, which now hung dull and lifeless against her skin.

Troy could almost see the power draining from her, and he could feel it pulsing into him through the sword.

Find a weakness and exploit it.

He lunged again, driving her back with the magical sword, and again slashed at the amulet. This time, he struck the chain, and the amulet fell from her neck onto the ground.

The sorceress spun away, ducking for cover behind a bush, her eyes scanning the sky.

A dragon dove toward her, and she lashed out at it with her spell.

Troy stepped in the way, blocking the spell with his sword. The dragon dodged and spewed fire at the sorceress. She erected a shield, but it was weak.

They were wearing her down.

Troy picked up the amulet and held it in his hand, changing the sword so it grew from the amethyst in the center instead of from the garnet.

"Enough!" he bellowed, his voice echoing across the field.

All eyes, dragon and human alike, turned to face him.

"It's over. I've won. You are not a goddess. You are just a pathetic sorceress who would rather destroy everything than find contentment in what you do have. But you're done. This is my land, these are my people, and I will not let you have them. Surrender."

The sorceress snarled and grasped all the magic she could, pulling it into herself. "If I cannot win, no one can," she hissed. The power she held exploded out from her.

Heat like fire scorched the earth, blackening the already dead and dying plants, burning Troy's skin. Wave after wave pulsed out, and still the sorceress maintained the spell.

She had to be stopped.

Troy formed the sword into a shield and took a step. It was like fighting against the strongest wind. His muscles ached and his feet burned from the blazing ground, but still he pushed forward, one step at a time, into the heart of the sorceress's spell.

He had one chance.

Find a weakness and exploit it.

He stepped into the circle inside the spell, within reach of her body.

She looked at him, startled at first, then turned a smile on him. "Don't you see? Together we could rule everything. Together we could be unstoppable! Join me."

Troy altered the magic into a sword again.

"I don't want to rule everything."

He plunged the sword into her chest.

She gasped and drew the magic back into herself, using it to try to Heal. Using the sword still inside her, Troy pulled all the magic she tried to absorb through the sword and into the amulet.

They fought for what seemed like an eternity, facing one another in an invisible contest, both pulling at the magic the other tried to wield, straining against the spells the other cast.

Slowly, though, Troy felt the sorceress's energy fading. He pulled harder. Find the weakness. Exploit it. With every moment, her strength lessened while his grew, until he drained the last of it from her and put it into the amulet.

The sorceress crumpled, her life draining with the magic that Troy took from her. She hit the ground and shattered into dust.

Troy recoiled with the force of the last of the magic snapping into the Amulet. The amulet burned in his hand, growing brighter until it was blinding, then exploding in a flash of light.

Troy stood there, staring at his empty hand. He didn't know how long he stood there before he started to realize that he could actually see his hand, even though the light was gone.

He looked up. The sky had a sickly gray pallor to it. Gray. Not black. Sickly, not thick and impenetrable

Around him, the magic users and dragons all became aware that the fight was over—they paused to breathe and congratulate one another on a battle well-fought. The cuffs fell off of those who were enslaved, and those who were part of the empress's army quickly surrendered when they realized the empress was dead. Some of the humans stared in awe at the dragons, until one by one, they also looked toward the sky.

The darkness faded more every moment, turning to light gray, then even lighter, almost as though it was an ordinary spring fog.

Ada hobbled up next to him, and he turned to look at her. "What next?"

The End

Ada took Troy's hand. "You did it."

He shook his head. "I didn't do it alone. I couldn't have done anything without all of you helping."

"Regardless." Ada chuckled. "You defeated the darkness. You saved the world. This is now the end of the Age. The new will begin."

"What does that mean?"

"I don't know, exactly. At the end of the last Age, the gods died off and people were left to rule themselves. If there are any prophecies for the next Age, I don't know them. All I can say is, the world will need rebuilding. If there are others alive in the world, they will come here. The magic here is strong, the people are strong—they will be drawn here to rebuild."

Troy nodded solemnly. "And we will help them."

The fog in the sky continued to thin, and after a few more moments, the sky turned blue. A short while after that, they could see the sun.

People began to gather around Troy. People and dragons. Even the dragons deferred to his leadership.

Altya was the first to bow and swear fealty.

Ada did not miss the admiring look in Troy's eyes as Altya explained her role as regent in his absence.

"Now that you're here," Altya said, "I am happy to follow your leadership, your Majesty. What should we do first?"

"We will begin here, in the North Village," he said. "Others are coming, and much like in the days when our nation was founded, we will accept refugees and build a society of peace."

"Will you still be the king?" someone asked.

"I don't know. If a king is needed, then I am happy to serve. But we have dragons, and those of us who have survived wish only to live in peace. The amulet—the relic which enabled my ancestors to rule—is gone, so perhaps such a thing will not be necessary in the coming Age."

Ada's mind drifted away from Troy's words of reassurance. She was so tired. Perhaps Troy was right. Perhaps they would no longer need a king—or a sorceress, bound to protect the land. Perhaps she could live out the rest of her days as a mortal human, in peace.

She had served well. Done her duty to her land and to her vow. She wouldn't change anything about the life she had lived, the sacrifices she'd made, the work she'd done to protect the kings and queens of Legerdemain throughout the last Age.

Only one thing lingered in her mind. Only one regret. One brief span in a thousand-year history. The one time she wanted something for herself and gave it up for her duty.

She inhaled deeply, allowing the ache in her heart that never went away to wash over her.

A dragon landed on the ground behind her.

At first, she didn't think much of it—she'd known all the dragons who went into the cairn for the Long Sleep. This one probably meant to catch up on all she had missed over the years, to reestablish a friendship.

Ada turned slowly, forcing a smile onto her face to greet the dragon.

She stopped, her jaw going slack.

A man rode the dragon's back. He was older now than the last time she'd seen him, his beard gray now instead of brown, the lines around his eyes deeper, but she would recognize him anywhere. The way his blue eyes sparkled. The way his mouth quirked up in that teasing smile.

She took a faltering step toward him. "Cornan."

He slid from the dragon's back and raced toward her, enveloping her in his arms.

Oh, those arms. She'd almost forgotten how it felt to be held by him. To feel his strength. To know that as long as she was with him, everything would be all right. In his arms, she was safe. Happy.

147

She didn't know when she'd started crying, only that Cornan held her tightly as she released all the emotion she'd kept buried for countless years. He ran his hands through her hair and kissed the top of her head until she finally caught her breath.

At long last, she pulled away far enough to look into his eyes. "How is this possible? I thought you must be long dead."

"I found the cairn. I found the portal and went in. I spent the last few dozen years living in a garden of sorts. Time seemed to flow normally, though when your prince released us, we discovered it had been much longer here." He stopped talking and let his gaze wander over her. "You're as beautiful as you ever were."

Ada laughed. "I am not. I'm old and..."

He silenced her with a kiss, and she melted into his embrace.

After a long moment, he released her and she leaned into his chest with a sigh.

All around them, people were setting to work repairing damage and settling in to the abandoned homes of the North Village.

"There is much to be done," Ada said.

Cornan hugged her tightly. "Yes. But this time, we will do it together."

The End

Dear Reader,

Thank you for reading **_The End_**. This series began as a collection of short stories that I published on the blog I used to write for, New Authors Fellowship (newauthors.wordpress.com). I had no idea when I first wrote _Rendezvous,_ the first story in _The Heir_, that I would grow to love this world so much and that the story would evolve into what it is today.

I am so excited to finish the stories in _The Amulet Saga_. This has been a wonderful journey, and I hope you had an enjoyable time embarking on it with me.

If you enjoyed this story, please tell a friend. Better yet, buy them their own copy.
You can also purchase The Heir, and The Defector, The Silver Shores, The Prophecy, The Sorceress, and The Beginning on Amazon.
Please also check out my full-length novels, as well.

The Breeding

Swimmer

I love connecting with readers. Please find me on Twitter (@avilyjerome), Instagram (@avilyjeromebooks), my website (www.avilyjerome.com), and Facebook (https://www.facebook.com/AvilyJ?fref=ts).

Yours truly,

Avily Jerome

About the Author

Avily Jerome is a writer and freelance editor. She spent five years as the Editor of Havok Magazine. Her short stories have been published in multiple magazines, both print and digital. She has judged several writing contests, both for short stories and novels, and she is a book reviewer for Lorehaven Magazine.

She loves all things SpecFic and writes across multiple genres. She is also a writing conference teacher and presenter, and she enjoys speaking to local writers' groups and going to SFF cons.

She is a wife and the mom of five kids. She loves living in the desert in Phoenix, AZ, and when she's not writing, she loves reading, spending time with friends, fencing, and experimenting with different art forms.

You can find her on her social media and on her website, at www.avilyjerome.com

www.ingramcontent.com/pod-product-compliance
Lightning Source LLC
Chambersburg PA
CBHW071920220626
47052CB00002B/429